AN ISLAND
TO DIE FOR

🙰

AN ISLAND
TO DIE FOR

&

Mark Ryno

ABSOLUTELY AMAZING eBOOKS

To My Mother, with love always.
To my buddy Hans, rest in peace.
And to my little buddy Rocco.
You were a good boy.

AN ISLAND
TO DIE FOR

CHAPTER 1

Ronnie.

HE KNEW WHAT HE LIKED. Always did. It was more often than not just the simple things in life. Good food. Good music. A good drink. A couple friends, not too many. Let's not get crazy.

A good whiskey sour was important to him too. He found most bars would screw it up. Too much sour and not enough whiskey, or the other way around. That's why he made them himself. At home.

He wasn't a big fan of going to bars. He'd been in a million of them all around the world and only liked a handful. There was a time when he'd most likely spent more money on spilt liquor than most people made in a year.

Most bars were either pretentious or way too loud or too fancy or just down right shitty. Actually the shitty bars were more to his liking, but not enough were he'd spend any amount of time there. Not these days.

Ronnie's days were spent in his tiny apartment under a sapodilla tree in Key West.

Key West. A town that bred inspiration. A town that had everything from Hemingway and Tennessee Williams and Robert Frost to ghosts, pirates and Sloppy Joe's. Key West was a place an author like Ronnie could take long naps, sometimes right after waking up. He'd drink. Maybe walk the dogs and take another nap. Somewhere in there he might write a chapter or two. Hemingway used to say all he wanted to do every day was write the perfect sentence.

Ronnie's goal was a bit less than that. His

sentences didn't have to be perfect. Most of his books were filled with very imperfect sentences. But people bought them anyway. Millions of them.

Stupid fucking people.

He hated most of them.

He loved their money.

Just not them.

It was one of the reasons Ronnie finally decided to move to Key West.

A place where a man like Ronnie could be left alone.

Left alone to write.

Or not.

Key West is a place where you can immerse yourself in the town or completely divorce yourself from it. Ronnie liked that.

Another big part of Ronnie's life in Key West was his dogs. Without those damn dogs he wouldn't know where he'd be. They kept him company and he was pretty sure they just plain understood him.

He'd take them out twice a day. As quickly as possible. The worst part of a dog walk down the street was when Betsy-Talks-A-Lot would catch you for a painful stop and chat. A stop and chat. Where you would be caught having a god-awful chat with a woman who had nothing to say.

She would mention, for the millionth time, how cute the dogs are.

She lived across the street.

The worst was the morning.

Even with his back turned she would, far too loudly yell, "Good Morning". A few times he would just ignore her. Look around like he saw or maybe heard something in the trees. Painful.

Who the fuck wants to talk in the morning? Ronnie was sure she had to be a psychopath.

The dogs would do their business, the older one

would always find some cat shit from the stray to gobble up. And then back inside. Back in the cool apartment.

Every day or two Ronnie would get a visitor. Because even assholes like Ronnie had needs.

Her name was Kelly. She was cute. Nice little body. Smelled good. Perky tits. Her face was maybe a 4, on a good day a 5. After half a dozen whiskey sours, a 6.

She would spend maybe an hour at the apartment. 20 minutes would be giving Ronnie some Grade A head. The rest of the time she'd pick up the place. Do a little cleaning. All the while either singing or chatting. Ronnie, of course, hated both.

But he figured if listening to her flapping her yap for 40 minutes was the price of a good blow job and a clean place then he was all the better for it.

Kelly was a bartender at night. A real shit hole called Dan's Bar and Dive Shop. It was 100% outside. They had these huge fans on either end that would blow everyone's smelly pits all around the place. You sat at these big picnic tables and the whole joint was under a huge sail.

The sail served a couple purposes. Number one it kept the sun out. Number two it kept the iguanas living in the trees above from shitting into your nachos.

Kelly loved her job there. Loved the place itself. Even the people. Especially the people. So much so that on her days off she'd hang out there.

She'd often regale Ronnie on her visits with stories of Drunken douchebags doing something douchey. Nine times out of ten they were all bullshit. But Kelly was kind of a rube. Not that bright.

Ronnie mostly let her have the stories as they were. But sometimes he couldn't help himself and he'd tell Kelly what stupid bullshit the story was.

On one particular visit, Kelly wasn't quite herself. It was easy to spot. She was quiet, which Ronnie didn't hate, but he knew it wasn't normal. Ronnie hated any kind of change or having any conversation out of the ordinary. But he knew he wouldn't get what he wanted until he asked.

"What's the matter?" (God how he hated conversations that started that way)

"Oh it's no big deal. Just some shit at work"

Whew Ronnie thought. No big deal is exactly the response he was hoping for.

His glee was short lived.

"I just don't get some people"

Oh Christ.

Ronnie thought there were a lot of people she didn't get.

The convo painfully would continue. He started to wonder if the dogs needed to go out.

"I mean, how come some people are so mean?"

Was this rhetorical, Ronnie thought.

"I dunno", Ronnie said with a shrug. Losing all interest in this conversation, this visit and now the whole damn day. It was all shot. Just because this broad couldn't talk it out with anyone else before she got here. Ronnie just wanted this to end and for her to go. Maybe by the next visit they could just go back to normal. Back to the jobby and some cleaning. He'd even take the singing at this point.

But there was no going back now. She had to get this shit off her chest and Ronnie was now the sounding board.

Little did Ronnie know that today, this visit would be the last time he'd see Kelly again. For a while.

The last time things were ever quite normal again.

CHAPTER 2

Familia.

KELLY WAS BORN AND RAISED in Key West. She was what locals considered a Conch. Like Konk on the head. That was an old Bahamian tradition when a baby was born a conch shell would be placed in the front yard. It was a tradition that continued even into modern day Key West.

She was born in the old marine hospital on A1A. She went to Key West High. And outside of some teenage and early twenties trouble, she had a pretty good reputation among other locals. She was well liked and known as someone that you could count on. She was a good conch. And believe it, there were lots of bad conchs.

Her family has been in Key West for several generations. They have roots in this little island town, and here like many places, that means something.

Her family also has seen its fair share of trouble. Kelly's father was arrested in the 1970's with about a dozen other conchs in an illegal Cuban cigar ring. Cuban cigars, even in Key West, were illegal. But when word got out that there were millions of dollars trading hands between Key West and Miami, it didn't take long before the Feds got involved.

In the early morning hours of September 14th, 1975, the Federal agents, in simultaneous separate raids, hit about 20 different cigar shops and bodegas around Key West.

Word traveled fast. It always does in a small town. And on a small island. Kelly's father, Uncle and 10 other men were arrested that day just in Key West and

24 more in Miami.

When the mainland news got ahold of the story, it was ugly for Kelly's family. It painted an awful picture of her father and uncle engaged in not only the illegal cigar trade, but in other drugs and prostitution and gambling. And there were whispers of the Miami/Cuban mafia.

Kelly's father made bail that day at the federal courthouse in Miami but never got close to getting back to Key West.

As he and his brother were pulling out of the courthouse, where they'd been for hours, 4 cars came quickly up the drive and surrounded the car and opened fire. After it was all said and done and those cars peeled out and away, the investigation revealed that there was somewhere in the neighborhood of 100 rounds fired into that car. They had said Kelly's dad and uncle were each hit with more than 3-dozen bullets.

So many in fact, Uncle Joe's head was nearly separated from his body. Her father didn't fare much better.

There was no denying it now. This was a mob business run by the mob and this was a mob hit.

A message. A message to all the other defendants that the main players were now taken out. In the driveway of the federal courthouse no less, and if they had talking in mind, they'd better think it over long and hard.

There was never one conviction outside of the players that got arrested that day. It never went any further. The message was received. Loud and clear.

As could be imagined, that was a horrible day for Kelly. Her entire family and a bad image day for Key West. It was a bad image still to this day. The idea that it was still a mob town and a good place for the mob to hang out or lamb.

To this day, Kelly and her entire family haven't lived it down. It comes up often at shithole bars all over town. Including the one that Kelly currently works at.

Sometimes people talking know it was Kelly's family and sometimes they don't.

It was always uncomfortable for her. She hated the stories and the looks and worst of all, the looks on faces when they found out her last name. That she was one of them. Family to those men that were brutally murdered in a mob hit in Miami.

But it was something that she lived with. The whole family had to live with it. But with Kelly, she was the only one who worked at a shit hole bar were people reveled in gossip and stories of the past. The stories everyone loved to tell. Everywhere. Murder. Mystery. Drugs and the Mafia.

Quite frankly, Ronnie often thought about the whole damn thing. It was one helluva story. He started to ask Kelly on a few different occasions about it but always backed out at the last second. He knew on some level that that was the very last thing she wanted to talk about.

But Kelly managed to keep her head up. Her mother did a good job keeping her focused and busy and active and most importantly, for the most part, out of trouble. Serious trouble anyway. She got popped a couple times for pot and once a drunk driving arrest, which in Key West was something she shared with most everybody. No one cared about the pot arrests either. This was, after all, a great pot town.

She decided after high school to travel the world. To see the mainland and everywhere else. To get off this goddamn island. She'd saved thousands of dollars, could've cared less about college and was itching to go explore the world.

Instead she fell in love. Love has a way of changing shit. Changing plans. And when men find out their women have money, at least some men, trouble usually follows.

Kelly never made it off the rock. She instead spent a whole lot of time trying to make a man happy.

She knows now that that's not where it's at, at all.

After a few years of dating and being mistreated by this asshole, he went fishing one day and never came back. Not in one piece anyway.

It was a boating accident. The asshole somehow got himself tangled up in the prop. Bad move.

Props love to eat assholes.

It was for the best.

Funny thing is, Kelly wasn't all that sad. She played it well at the funeral and all but deep down, she was relieved. He really was a fucking asshole. She didn't love him. Hadn't for a long time. She stayed, more than anything else, because she didn't want to be alone. She hated being alone.

So now broke, with no chance in the foreseeable future of leaving the island, she went to work. She worked for just about everybody on the island. Everything from the greasy rooster, actually a much better restaurant than you might think, to a car dealer to receptionist at a local radio station to substitute teacher ... you name it. She worked all over town.

But she liked bar tending. She was pretty good at it. Her Dad worked at bars around town for a good portion of his life and he taught her a whole hell of a lot. Taught her to make drinks that no one ever heard of and all of the most popular drinks too.

He made it fun for her and when she'd get it right, he would reward her with a little piece of hard candy, which she loved. It was actually some of the best memories with her Dad and was the main reason she even got into bartending. While she did all of those other jobs, she always tended bar on the side.

It was how she met Ronnie. He said she was the only bar chic in town that knew how to make a whiskey sour right ... every single time. Anyone, Ronnie said, can make a drink right once, but a good bartender made it right every time.

Kelly had to spend some time at OceanView for a little while after all that shit with her Dad. Her cheese sort of slipped of her cracker so to speak. She needed about 6 weeks in there to sort it all out.

She came out a little better but was still a little touched. She was never the same really. Thank God there was no Internet then, pictures of the crime scene would've made it to her eyes at some point.

Kelly really was a good girl. She always tried her best to do the right thing. She had a good heart. But ... she was a little fucked up.

Every once in a blue moon, Ronnie would notice some weird shit about Kelly. It might be something she would say. It might be a reaction to something the dogs did. It could be anything. Something would click inside her at strange times and she would just react bizarre.

It didn't bother Ronnie. It fascinated him.

She might fly off the handle because there was no milk in the house. Or, there was garbage to be taken out. Or one of the dogs, God forbid, squeaked out a little dog fart.

So, it was just a lot of little weird shit like that that Ronnie would notice and sort of store away somewhere in the back of his mind. It was a tiny bit unsettling, but nothing he became super concerned about.

Until the day that Kelly was just different. The day

she was wondering why people were the way they were. Of course, that's always a bad sign. Ronnie was a firm believer that thinking too god damn much was the real danger all over the world. Too much thinking leads to fear and fear leads to a box underground much much sooner than expected.

"How come people are so mean?" was the question. Ronnie didn't know the answer and quite frankly didn't give a fuck. He didn't deal with many people, so who fucking cares.

One of the great things about having a few bucks is not worrying about shit that normal people worried about. But the question she asked clearly meant a lot to her. It was not rhetorical. She wanted an answer.

"How come people are so mean?"

Christ. Where was this going?

CHAPTER 3

Crusty Drunk.

SO THERE THEY SAT. At the foot of the bed. Ronnie with a collared pink button down shirt and Kelly with too small cut off jean shorts and this little tiny tank top that really showed off those cute little tits. Her hair, which was a very attractive brown/black/red color, was pulled back into a loose bun. Kelly had beautiful eyes. Considering how the rest of her face looked like 40 miles of bad road, those eyes and those eyelashes made Ronnie's heart skip a bit every so often.

"Huh, why?"

"Kiddo, I'm not sure. People are just assholes most of the time. What are we talking about here anyway?"

God, he wished he didn't ask that question. Maybe this could've gone away. But not now. Now, because of dummy Ronnie, there's a follow up question and now soon to come, a most likely completely ignorant statement from Kelly.

Or worse ... another question.

"You're right! People are such assholes."

"Babe, help me out here. What's going on?"

"Well, today at Dan's Jack said something that really upset me. I mean, I don't think he meant it. He had a few rum and cokes in him, but it hurt my feelings anyway."

"What the fuck did that stupid crusty old drunk say? And why would you let that dickhead say anything that would upset you?"

"It was just so ... out of left field!"

Oh Christ Ronnie thought, this is going way too slow. He also thought about her nipples poking through that tank top and how much he wanted her to go down to man-land right now.

"Well???"

"He told me today that my father wasn't killed after all. He told me he heard it was my uncle and someone else in that car. Not Daddy."

"How could that possibly be?" he asked.

There had been this conspiracy theory around Key West for years that Kelly's dad just vanished instead of being killed. That just her Uncle was killed. That her dad walked in one door of the courthouse and out the back door never to be seen again.

"He's in Costa Rica."

Or

"He's in Cuba."

Or some shit like that.

But Jack. Well Jack really was an asshole made even more so when he was watered down with booze.

"He told me he knows for a fact that Daddy is alive and in Cuba alright. He told me he went there to get away from it all. To cool down. To let it all cool down."

Ronnie thought about it and said "Hon, you know what a classless drunk Jack is. How could he possibly remember what happened 30 years ago when he has a hard time remembering what happened 30 seconds ago.

"He said he knew who was sending him money to keep him alive. He said Daddy was remarried. He said he saw him just 2 months ago, Ronnie! TWO MONTHS!"

Kelly continued as if she were just letting it all come out of her brain. Like she wanted to get it all out to someone before she forgot everything that dickhead Jack said. Ronnie had never seen Kelly this upset. This ragged. This wrung out. She was losing it.

"Alright, alright. Calm down. We're gonna figure all

this out, kiddo."

Ronnie wrapped his arms around her. Trying to comfort her, but really only able to think about 2 things.

1) what the fuck is going on with Kelly's dad? and

2) would it be bad if in her current state and now in Ronnie's arms, he would gently push her head down towards his crotch?

He didn't know the answer to the first question but the answer to the second question just hit him. Literally.

"Ronnie!" she slapped his leg hard. "How can you even think I'd want to fool around right now?"

Too obvious Ronnie guessed. He may or may not have been already pushing her head down while he was thinking about it. Too soon he thought.

"Ronnie I got a bad feeling about this. I think I'm going to be sick."

Kelly ran to the bathroom and let it all out. She was sick. She was sick to think her father would do this to her Mom. She was sick to think there was another Mom and maybe other siblings. Half siblings. This was all just so fucked up she thought. As she heaved and heaved she continued to think about her dad relaxing in Cuba with his second wife. Drinking a piña colada or some shit. His new wife rubbing his shoulders or fanning him with those huge palm leaves.

Ok, maybe not that last one. But she was thinking about him and it. It being the whole god damn situation. The very thought her Dad alive was really sort of bittersweet. A part of her was so thrilled that her Dad wasn't killed and the other half was kicking him in the balls over and over again.

CHAPTER 4

A Good Boy.

FRANKIE ALVAREZ WAS BORN in Key West at a time when the little island was still trying to find itself. Somewhere between shipwrecking and before tourism really kicked into high gear.

The island was a lot different in those days. But it was good. Simple for sure. But good. A little lonely. Maybe even a tad secluded. But good.

A small town where everyone truly knew your name. And your parents name. And their parents name too. If someone caught you fucking off in town, they wouldn't hesitate to grab you by your collar and give you the what for. And before you would even get home your Mom would already know what happened. You couldn't get away with shit.

Frankie for the most part, was like all the other boys on the island. A real outdoor kid who loved to fish and swim and be out on the water in a boat. Key west was an outside kind of place. There wasn't much if any TV in those days and with about 300 days of sunshine and beautiful weather, kids pretty much stayed outside all day and into the night.

The only thing your Mom wanted was you home for dinner at 5 o'clock. Period. No questions asked.

All the kids ate dinner at 5.

What you did before that and what you'd be up to after didn't really make much difference. But at 5 o'clock you were at the dinner table with clean hands with your Mom and Dad eating a big plate of something good.

You could always smell what Frankie's mom was

cooking all the way down the street. She was known for her cooking. She had fed just about everyone on the island at one point or another. She'd be the first person to bring a plate to someone who was sick. She'd always have something for the bake sale. You name it. She would be in the kitchen, it seemed like, 24 hours a day. Dinner was an event. The perfect way to wrap up the day. You could always count on Cuban bread and black beans and rice and then some kind of meat in there. Always good.

Dessert would be fresh fruit from any one of the fruit trees on the street with a splash of sugar and whip cream on top.

Then ... it was back outside. No one in Key West ever heard of relaxing and letting things digest. Especially if you were an adventurous kid on a cool island where there was always something to explore.

Frankie did well at school, even though he got his ears pulled from time to time. He always got good grades and never really tried too hard.

He was just a smart kid. Was from the day he was born they said. He was so smart that he was the kid all the other kids looked up too. By the time Frankie was 13, he had already started to grow into a very handsome strapping young man. A natural athlete. A natural baseball player. Which in Key West, being good at baseball when you were 13 was about all that matter. To everyone!

Baseball had always been kind of big at Key West High. Football too, but baseball was different.

They started kids out early. Mostly to keep them out of trouble, but the kids every season were better and better. There were a couple guys who almost made it to the big leagues but never quite got there.

But Frankie? Frankie had potential, they all said. The high school coaches were already watching him. Talking to him. Trying to keep him on track until they could suit him up for the high school team. At this point Frankie was only in 7th grade, they need him in at least his freshman year to play varsity. But a freshman playing varsity baseball was almost unheard of. But if anyone could do it, it was Frankie Alvarez.

He was a good-looking kid too. The knocks on the door never stopped. Girls looking for Frankie. The calls didn't stop either. His looks didn't exactly run in the family. He was kind of an exception because no one in the Alvarez family was very good looking.

But Frankie managed to stay out of trouble, no easy task here. He worked hard. His father had a little gas station that he worked at in the summer and after school. He actually got pretty good at tune-ups and shit like that. He also was the fill up boy for cars that wanted a top off on the gas.

The island loved him.

He was a sweet, polite, good looking, smart, gifted, natural athlete kind of kid. All American even.

And a great personality and pretty funny for a kid.

He'd keep the old men that would hang around the station laughing while he mimicked old ladies that came in. Some hunched over or limping or just a crab. Frankie had all the imitations down pat, and the old boys loved it. They would try and talk Frankie into staying longer. He was that much fun to be around.

Sometimes you forgot that he was just 13 years old.

Frankie made his way into high school and as a freshman he was on the varsity baseball team as the star pitcher. And man, what an arm!

He was a star every season. Right up until he was a senior.

That's when things kind of just changed.

Frankie changed a little.

Maybe it was coming out the other side of puberty or the fact that he was seriously into his beautiful girlfriend. Something.

But as Frankie started his senior year he was just a little less funny. A tad less outgoing. A lot more serious and a bit easy to fly off the handle.

Everyone noticed but didn't really say anything. Just kind of chalked it up to hormones. Growing pains.

Then one day, Frankie just disappeared.

Gone.

It shook the town up. Police and firemen and just about every able-bodied local spent endless hours looking for him. Looking for some clue as to where he went. There was no reason for him to just walk away. He had a good life. Had it all going his way. He had planned to join the fire department right out of high school and the town loved that.

This didn't make any sense at all.

After 3 days and 3 nights, people just started to think he either left the island and went up the road or, quietly, they thought his body might wash onto shore someday soon.

There were only two options really.

Gone or dead.

Kind of the way the island thought about things like this. Fucked.

Months went by and there where no calls, no letters, nothing. Frankie's parents never gave up looking. Even driving to the mainland themselves, which was rare. They never stopped.

The town never really did either. He was a tough kid to just let go. Nobody wanted to believe the worst. But there were whispers all around the island.

Some folks said he killed himself. Out in the water somewhere.

Some folks said he drowned.

Some folks said he was up the road somewhere. Off the rock.

And still other folks said it was another girl that got

him all mixed up.

But nobody really knew.

And then, one day, just like that, Frank was back.

Back at the gas station. Working.

Little by little what seemed like thousands of neighbors and residents of the island crossed over that rubber hose and you heard the bell ding. They wanted a look at Frank.

Frankie.

Sonofabitch, there he was alright. He looked just the same. Sort of.

He seemed just a bit off. Seemed like he was often staring off into space. Moved a little slower. Didn't smile as easy. Everybody felt it and some said it.

But that one day. That one day when he came back, it was a good day for Frankie. He got so many hugs and kisses he couldn't help but smile. The town was welcoming Frank home. The only way this town knew how ... with love.

Sitting off to the side while all of this was happening, this Frankie homecoming of sorts, sat Frank Sr.

Senior was watching his boy. He knew something wasn't quite right. He could feel it. A dad has a way of knowing when something isn't quite right with his boy. He watched everyone hugging and squeezing and kissing his boy. And he watched Frankie's face. Something not right.

It was emotion. Frankie just didn't seem to have much emotion on his face or in the way he moved and seemed.

Senior had no idea what Frank had done or where he'd been, but he got a sick feeling inside that it wasn't something very damn good.

CHAPTER 5

Questions.

FRANK'S YOUNGER BROTHER also was watching his brother. Wondering what happened. Joe hadn't really stopped crying ever since Frankie came home. In those days, in that place, there was nothing more important to a young kids life than his big brother. Joe never broke down while they were looking. He was strong the whole time. But when Frankie just knocked on the family homes door one night, Joe lost it. He fell onto his knees and started sobbing. He was holding onto Frankie's legs. Sobbing.

Frank Senior and his wife, Charlotte were holding on and not letting Frankie move.

They couldn't let go if they wanted too.

Of course Charlotte got busy in the kitchen after about 2 hours of holding onto her son.

She cooked up a big meal and everyone sat down at the table.

It started out very uncomfortable. No one really knew what to say. So, they ate. Everyone stared at Frankie. Waiting to hear his voice. He hadn't really said anything in the last couple hours.

Charlotte couldn't take her eyes away from her son and couldn't stop smiling. She was happy. She didn't care where he was she was just happy he was here now. Eating her dinner at her table.

Joe was still weeping. He was also very very happy.

But Senior? He was also happy he was home but also had a whole helluva lot of questions to ask. He absolutely cared what the fuck his boy had been up too. But Senior had to wait. Had to bide his time. Wait for the right opportunity. Maybe even let his oldest boy get some sleep. But at some point and some point soon, Senior had some god damn questions that needed to be answered.

But the answers would have to wait. It didn't take long after a quiet dinner, that Frankie said, very quietly, if it was ok with everyone he'd like to go to bed.

His Momma said to of course go ahead and get some rest. She said they could wait till morning to talk more.

As Frank and Charlotte watched outside the door, Frankie fell asleep. His parents watched. Then looked at each other incredulously. Like to say, "What the fuck just happened?" Or "What the fuck has he been up to?" Or "Where the fuck has he been?" But answers tomorrow. Maybe.

If Frankie was up to it.

The next morning rolled around and by the time he came down the stairs he could smell the mother of all breakfasts being prepared as if the Queen herself was coming.

Frankie half expected there to be those long horns the British used when they went fox hunting to be played.

He quietly sat down and started to eat the plate his mother had prepared for him. It was quiet. Could've heard a pin drop.

Senior was the last to come down the stairs. They knew when he was up because when they heard peeing coming from upstairs, a big fog horn fart would be close behind ... pun intended.

Everyone was still very happy. But Senior looked like he hadn't slept much. Charlotte and little Joey felt like something bad was about to happen.

As Senior sat down next to Junior, he looked at him for quite a while. Watching him eat. Then someone finally broke the silence.

It was Senior.

"Son, I am so glad you're home. I love you so much. We're all really grateful that our prayers were answered. But I got to ask this ... Where the fuck have you been?!"

Frankie kept his head down, concentrating on his plate.

After what felt like several minutes, Frankie looked up, and with zero emotion said, "I went and saw some friends up on the mainland. I needed to get away for a little bit."

Now Senior looked not so happy that Junior was home. Very not so happy.

Months of feeling like he'd lost his son came to a head. Right there where all this food, enough for a small army, sat.

"Son, you got to tell me ... where the fuck were you and what have you been doing the last few months? Was it a girl?"

Frankie finally looked up and with a mouth full of breakfast said, "No. No girl. No nothing. Just wanted to get away"

"Get away from what?!" said Senior. "Tell me what you had to get away from. You've got a job. You've got a place to lay your head. What was it? Or maybe I should be asking, what IS it?"

Frankie never stopped eating. He nodded his head to the questions that weren't there. He was acting like a punk kid. Sort of typical ... for every teenager ... except Frankie maybe.

᠍᠍᠍ 🦢

CHAPTER 6

After All We've Been Through.

KELLY ALVAREZ WALKED OUT of the bathroom feeling a tiny bit better. She felt better to have that evil out of her stomach and system but it didn't take long, maybe 30 seconds, to remember why she rushed in there to begin with.

She started to feel not so much sick this time, but just ... sad.

Confused.

Mad.

Ronnie had been lying on the couch when she came out. Staring at the ceiling. He'd been thinking now how much he wanted Kelly to be gone. How much he wanted this drama to be over. No matter how interesting this story was, and it was fucking interesting, all the tears and throw up really turned him off from the whole goddamn thing.

He really was a selfish prick.

Really only ever thought about himself.

Maybe that's why he has 3 ex wives.

He never was one to have a lot of feelings.

He never was one who cared too much. About anyone else especially.

Ronnie was what some called cold. Unfeeling.

Others just called him a fucking asshole.

As Kelly sat on the edge of the bed, Ronnie sat up and stared at her. Wondering what the fuck else to say. He didn't have to wonder long.

She went first.

"Ronnie, I'm really scared. What if all of this is true? What then?"

"Well, how do we prove it? I mean, I don't even know where to start!" he sort of sarcastically replied.

"Cuba? Maybe in Cuba? Maybe we do a little digging and go to Cuba to investigate?"

"WE? You got to be shitting me, Kelly. You want to go to Cuba and look for a needle in the haystack? You even realize how hard it would be to find a 70 something year old man that's been hiding in Cuba for 30 years?!"

Kelly was not deterred.

"You've got a couple bucks right? And time to help. Wouldn't you like to know? Like to know the story and the truth?"

Kelly had him there. The answer was yes. Of course, yes. He'd love to know. The problem was all the effort it would take to find out. From all the packing to the trip itself and the heat and all that fucking effort. This was literally something that could take an undetermined amount of time and who knows how much Goddamn money.

That's where it all broke down for Ronnie. Not to mention being with Kelly non-stop for what? A week? Maybe 2? Maybe a month or more?!

Oh Christ! The very thought. What the fuck would they even talk about and do. 3 meals a day together. Doing everything together. No. This was a bad idea that was about to get even worse.

"You wouldn't help me with this? After all we've been through?!"

And there was the ace. The old "after all we've been through" card. She pulled it out and slapped it on the table. There it was. In front of Ronnie. For the world to see. That card has ruined more men's lives than almost any others.

"Yea, we've been through a lot, Kelly. But Christ, this is a big deal. We don't even know where to start!"

Kelly was staring back at Ronnie, actually through Ronnie. And then it hit her, "Jack! We find out more from Jack. He said he knew right where Daddy is. We could pump him for everything he knows and maybe even take him with us!"

"Are you fucking high?" Ronnie said, "Do you honestly think I want to be on a plane or a boat with that specimen? And then be in Cuba for god knows how long, living with him??!! KILL ME NOW!"

Kelly was glaring at Ronnie now. "It's the only way! Jack is the only one who knows where Daddy is! He's the only one that can help me! Please Ronnie, help me with this. You're the only one I want with me on this."

Then it was Ronnie's turn to be what everyone close to him knew he was, a dick. "Yea, cause you'll need my money."

He said it under his breath, but it was after all a tiny apartment. She heard it all right. And the look that came over her face is one Ronnie will never forget. He instantly regretted saying it and instantly knew he'd hurt her. Deep.

"FUCK YOU, RONNIE! After all this time together, you think I give a shit about your money?! Is that what you really think??!"

Ronnie couldn't find the words to respond. He didn't have too.

"You know what, Ronnie. I'm done with this. You could've just said no flat out. You didn't have to insult me. I'll do this without you! I should've known if it were anything about anyone else besides you you wouldn't be interested. Fuck off, Ronnie."

As Kelly headed to the door, Ronnie jumped up and blocked her way. He wasn't thinking right at this moment. He only wanted to apologize. But it went south, as far as he was concerned.

"Get the fuck out of my way, Ronnie."

Ronnie held his ground, "where you gonna go?"

"I'm going to Dan's and I'm going to talk to Jack and then I'm going to Cuba. I gotta figure this out. And it looks like I'll be doing it alone."

With that she shoved Ronnie out of the way. Hard enough where he slipped back down onto the couch. By the time he managed to get back off the couch, she was out the door, down the steps and onto her little red scooter, and then gone.

Gone.

CHAPTER 7

Captain Jack.

KELLY WAS CRYING BEFORE she got to the intersection. She was hurt. Deeply. The one person on the island she thought she could trust basically just told her to go fuck herself and your whole father deal. She wasn't only hurt she was stunned. Like a hard slap across the face.

She had been sort of "with" Ronnie for a long time and just assumed he would support her. She assumed he would be there for her. She thought the old saying was true when you assume.

As Kelly got onto the Boulevard she was already moving onto what she would do next. She HAD to find her father. No other way around it. But she didn't know anything about Cuba, other than it was 90 miles away. She didn't know if you could fly or take a ferry, nothing.

All of it was going to come down to Jack.

Jack was an old disgusting asshole drunk BUT he owned a charter boat and still went to Cuba on fishing charters all the time. Not as much as he used to, but he still did it.

She turned around in the Burger King parking lot and headed to Dan's. She knew Jack would be there. He was always there. He had nothing else to do. God knows he didn't have any friends anymore. He burned them all over the years. He'd be sitting on that same stool at the end of the bar, by himself, just like always.

Jack had been around a long time in Key West. He was a boy here towards the end of Hemingway's time in town, right around 1940. He'd always been a charter boat captain as long as anyone could remember. He was known around town as Captain Jack. No one really knew how old he was. Some say 70's and others say 80's. He looked 143.

All that sun, salt, rum and camel cigarettes has a way of fucking up a man's face and body. He had stringy white hair with a stringy little beard with a rubber band bunching it together at the bottom. He had one ear ring in the shape of an old pirates sword in his left ear. He wore an old skull ring that looked like you'd have to cut his finger off to remove it. He wore the same jeans and t-shirt just about every single day. And he always had the same pair of old beat up boat shoes on, with no socks mind you. His ensemble was topped off with the most worn out captain's hat on his head you'd likely ever seen. It had small holes all around it and an anchor on the front of it. It most likely used to be blue. But blue passed this hat by a long long time ago. Now it was some weird mix of gray and black.

Jack couldn't have weighed more than 135 pounds, soaking wet and was maybe five foot eight.

A small, dirty old man. Who sat at the same bar, in the same seat every single goddamn day.

When the day comes that Old Captain Jack doesn't show up at Dan's, that's the day you better check his boat for odd smells.

He lives out on the hook as they say in Key West. He's got his 35-foot live-aboard sailboat anchored just a little south of the island, near a little place known as Wisteria Island.

It was a shitty little undeveloped island that a lot homeless people would camp on. It was dangerous to be on that island, especially at night.

But being on a boat wasn't as bad. Jack had been anchored in the same spot for years. No one bothered him and most liked him. He had a little dinghy that he would putt-putt into the island on every day. And then hop off, tie her down, hop on his old beat up bicycle and ride her over to Dan's. It was a long slow ride. He had it timed out perfectly so that he'd always be the first one there, as soon as they opened, every day.

Maybe once a week, he'd take a group fishing on his charter boat that was docked at the city marina. Maybe once a week.

He worked when he wanted too. Which wasn't very often. But he knew how much money he needed to get by and so that's how much, or how little, he worked. He didn't owe anybody a dime and had no bills. Anyone could live on the hook for free. Of course life would've been a lot easier for ol Jack if he had some friends. He didn't. People treated him like a disease on the island. Avoided him at all costs. He was just a mean old stinkin' creep that managed at one point or another, over the course of a few decades, to Piss just about everyone off.

And on a small island, it doesn't take much to make it through the whole population. And of course like any small town, once people knew you were a fucking dick head, word just kept getting around.

So it was no surprise then when Kelly pulled into Dan's gravel parking lot that Jack was exactly where she knew he'd be.

She walked right up to him and without as much as one word greeting him she said, "I want you to take me to see my Dad!"

Jack looked up and when he saw it was Kelly, his eyes opened wide and he said, "Whoa whoa, little girl. It ain't that easy!"

"I don't care how hard it is, I want you to take me to Cuba so I can see my Daddy!!"

She was standing firm. Eyes still a little wet. She

had her hands on her hips and her lips were tight. She meant business.

"Listen, girl. I ain't going to Cuba anytime soon and even if I was going I ain't going for free ... for nobody!"

Kelly leaned in a half step closer. Looked ol Jack straight in the eyes and said, "Did I say you'd be going for free? I got money."

Jack raised his head off the bar all the way now. He was starting to see the possibility of a pretty good payday. How much money does this little broad have, he thought. Maybe this could be a good thing for him too. An easy trip. One passenger. Big money.

"Oh ya got money do ya? Well, that ain't no trip for a little girl."

Kelly got as close as possible to Jack without having to smell him. Leaned in within an inch of his face and said, "If you call me a little girl again I'm gonna kick you in your old saggy fucking nuts so hard they're gonna stick to that stupid earring of yours! I'm going to Cuba to find my father and whether you like it or not you're the one taking me there."

At this point Jack knew he was losing this battle. Of course he wasn't putting up much of a fight. He was an old man. An old drunk at that.

Why fight?

"Alright, little Missy. For me to take you to Cuba is gonna cost you $2,000. Ya got $2,000 missy?"

Kelly pulled out of her purse ten one hundred bills. "This is all I got and you're going to take it."

Jack thought about it for a minute. $1,000 was a lot of money for him. He could do a lot with it. Mostly drink it, but if he was smart he could make it last. Do some work around home. Fill the place with some groceries for a change.

"Alright, I'll take your $1000. But I'm getting you

down there and back. I'm gonna point out the area I last saw him and then I'm going down below and drink and sleep until you come back. I'm not a private detective. And when we're on my boat, you'll keep your mouth shut and do what I tell ya. Got it?!"

"That's fine. I just want to get there. When can we leave?"

Jack said, "Well, I suppose we can leave first thing in the morning. She's already to go. All fueled up. I actually had a charter today that cancelled on me, those fuckers. So, let's say 6am tomorrow. And not a minute past or you can have your money back and stick it up your ass!"

"Watch it, dickhead. We're not on that boat yet. I'll be at the city marina at 6am sharp. Be sober!"

CHAPTER 8

A Sweet Girl.

RONNIE HAD TRIED TO CALL KELLY a few times with no luck. For the first time in a long time he regretted how everything went down with them. He didn't feel bad, mind you. Just wished it had gone a different way. Ronnie hated shit like this. Hated change. Hated confrontation. All of it. This was why Ronnie stayed to himself. It's why Ronnie moved to Key West. It's why Ronnie was banging a slow broad who poured drinks for a living.

No worries.

Nothing to think about.

He had the same routine every day and liked it.

He did the same thing every day because it was comfortable.

And any day that Ronnie could get through without so much as seeing another human being was a big Fucking win.

But Kelly, was a sweet girl. She meant well. She tried to do the right things. She was happy, almost to a fault. But Ronnie always thought that happy people were real fucking assholes. Smart people were downright miserable every day. Smart people knew there had to be something bigger than this. Something better. Smart people often asked whether this was as good as it got. Happy people didn't think about those things. Happy people thought about shit like sunflowers and rainbows all Fucking day. Ronnie was pretty sure of it.

Happy people annoyed the shit out of Ronnie.

He sat in his apartment and thought about Kelly. What's she going to do now? She's not thinking right. Is she going to do something rash? It's not like Kelly was an adventurous soul or anything. Where could she go? What could she possibly do?

Ronnie made another whiskey sour. His fourth of the day and it was just a tick past one in the afternoon. He sat back and puffed on his macanudo. Head up as he blew a thick cloud of smoke above his head. Feet up on the coffee table. This was him being contemplative. He got a lot of shit done this way. A lot of thinking in this pose.

Sipped his sour. Perfect, he thought. No one can make them better than him, he mused. He looked at his dogs who were on the bed, sprawled out across the whole thing, staring at him. Ronnie hated when his dogs stared at him. It freaked him out. They would sometimes watch his every move. Creepy.

As he took another gulp of whiskey sour, he went back to thinking about that whole deal with Kelly. Thinking about what happened and what was said. He was concentrating on her words.

Thinking about her plan to go to Cuba. He thought how stupid that was. What good could possibly come out of that? Wasn't there an old saying about sleeping dogs? He didn't understand why she had to do this. Why it was so important now. And it all might be bullshit. She's listening to an old drunk asshole. That's whose word she was taking. How much could he know? The story of seeing Frank could've been from 20 years ago. Not two months.

Then Ronnie thought about what he would do in the same situation. He thought about his Dad who died in 2004. Fucking cancer. He thought about anything he would do to bring him back. He thought about how he would react if after all these years of thinking his dad was dead, somebody said they saw him.

That's when it finally hit Ronnie.

He believed there would be nothing to stop him from finding out.

CHAPTER 9

Kelly Knew. She Always Knew.

KELLY KNEW. SHE ALWAYS KNEW. There had been rumblings about it ever since he got back, and ever since she'd been born. They tried to keep it from her, but she knew. Kids have a way of finding shit out about their parents. Especially when they've all lived in the same town their whole lives.

Frankie left town for one reason and one reason only ... money. Gobs and gobs of it.

At the height of Frankie's popularity he was approached one day after a baseball game in Key West. A man who said he knew his family.

He congratulated Frankie on the win and asked what his plans for the future were. When Frankie said he was still looking things over and thinking about his options, the man said he'd like to talk to him about one option maybe he hadn't thought about. An option that could make him more money than any other.

As an 18-year-old kid, that sounded awful damn good. Frankie really didn't have many options after all. As good of an athlete as he was, truth is no pro scout is coming all the way to Key West in those days unless you were Pete Rose or Babe Goddamn Ruth.

So when a mysterious man in a suit and tie approaches you and says things like "more money than any other option", he was open to the conversation. After Frankie showered and changed, he met the man in the parking lot where his Lincoln was parked. In those days, young men didn't worry about things like a kidnapping or anything bad happening to them. It was almost unheard of.

The man in the suit said hello and opened the door for Frankie.

He gave him a ride to the old Dairy Queen up the road on Stock Rock, which almost no one ever went too and was completely empty. They sat at a boot in the back and the man in the suit started to explain.

"So, Frank, is it ok if I call you Frank?"

"Everyone calls me Frankie."

"Alright Frankie. I got a little offer for you that can make you a very wealthy young man. An offer that only you can know about. I have an associate in Miami who knows you very well, but that you probably don't know at all. His name is George Alvarez. He's in the family. You probably never heard of him because your family turned its back on him a long time ago."

Frankie was surprised to hear that his family would turn their backs on anyone, especially family. What the fuck could he have done to be disowned? In this family?

"Why would my family turn its back on him?" Frankie asked. "My family doesn't do shit like that."

"Well, they did at least once that we know of for sure," said the man in the suit.

"Why? Why would they do that?"

"Well for starters, George was a bad kid. Always getting into trouble and causing trouble. Your family was at its wits end. They didn't know how to control him and how to keep him out of trouble. They just figured he was a bad seed. Families thought that in those days. Your family sent him to Miami, by force, to a boy's home there. A place where he could get strict teaching and a place where he would be put under control and taught how to be a respectful man. He was a lot of trouble. He could never get his shit together. So his parents brought him to the home in Miami. A nice place where not so nice young men came to be changed. Turned into good young men. Then, when that was complete, they'd go back home. Problem was, George was one of the only kids ever where the program didn't take. Maybe he was too smart for it or maybe too dumb for it, but it didn't work. He got a lot worse. Meaner."

Frankie was leaned in on his elbows listening to every word. His mouth was wide open and his eyes were wide. "I can't believe this."

"Believe it, kid. It's all true. So, George got too much for the program to handle. He was kicked out, first kid ever. He knew he couldn't go home, so he ended up on the street. Started hustling and stealing and doing whatever he could to survive."

"In Miami in those days, a kid could make it on the street. He could sleep on the beach safely and make enough money to eat by robbing tourists during the day, if you were good. And George was good. He slowly managed to get his own place and get off the beach at night. He met another street kid named Manny and the two became inseparable. Pulling jobs all over town."

"Now at the same time, the outfit from Chicago was starting to muscle its way into Miami. They got sick of the cold and also saw the potential of a town that was just starting to build up. It didn't take long for George to get noticed. He got picked up one day by a couple of men with pushed in noses and they took him to an old office building."

"They sat him down and offered him a job. Running numbers for the outfit. Easy job. $500/week. Period. George took that job in a second and started making a lot of money for a kid, let alone an adult. Wasn't long before they had him doing bigger and bigger jobs."

"One night he was out working, collecting money,

and got into it pretty good with the guy he was collecting from. A guy a lot bigger too. During the fight, George was getting the worst of it, he reached over to his right and saw a lead pipe nearby, he managed to grab it and then went to town on this kids head. He hit him so many times and so hard the pipe got bent. He had a problem with anger and once he got going he couldn't stop."

Frankie couldn't believe this story! It was crazy!

"After that, the outfit had even more respect for George but he had to lay low for awhile. They sent him to Chicago to work there. And while he was in Chicago, he just became bigger and bigger. More and more successful. His name started getting around town. People started calling him who were friends of the outfit for jobs all over town. George never said no. He took them all. Whatever the job was and whatever the job paid. He got quite a reputation. At some point, things cooled down in Miami and George went back to Miami. By the time he came back, he was a big fucking deal. Everyone knew who George Alvarez was. And everyone knew he was a guy not to be fucked with.

At one point a deal came through that the boys in Chicago thought was perfect for George. A job in another country. A little place just a small hop from Miami ... Cuba. George was asked to go to Cuba and set up a cigar shop or two. He did it. Over the years he became very successful and feared all over Cuba. He became known as a man that would get things done and as a man who did what he said he was going to do. After just a few short years, George was pulling down millions, had dozens of cigar shops, was involved in selling drugs and even had a couple nightclubs. Of course, he would be sure to send plenty of it back home. Not all of it, of course, but a good size cigar box full, or two."

Frankie sat here in this shit hole Dairy Queen listening to this strange man in a black suit and tie telling him the wildest shit he'd ever heard. He couldn't say a word. He just listened.

Suddenly, after all this talk and all these stories, Frankie had a thought. An important question.

"How do you know all this? I mean, it sounds like you were there or something."

The man in the suit looked at Frankie and said, "Always a thinker. Too god damn smart for your own good. A typical Alvarez. I WAS there, kid. I'm your big brother, George."

CHAPTER 10

Anxiety.

KELLY SHOWED UP RIGHT ON TIME. 6am sharp. Off in the distance she could see Jack on the boat. He was working, more like delegating, to his two deck hands on what to do. He was wearing the same clothes shoes and hat that he always wore. Kelly always wondered why he never smelled.

He should have. He was always so filthy looking. His look was smelly. Bad enough.

She climbed onto to the boat and said good morning to the three. None of them responded or even offered to help her on. Chivalry, as it turned out, was dead.

Jack looked her way and said, "You're a little late, missy!"

Kelly was not late. "I got here right at 6, just like you said."

"I wanted to leave at 6."

Kelly already had her fill of Jack and they hadn't even pushed away yet.

"Well you didn't say that. You said arrive at 6."

Jack gave her some sort of grump noise and turned back to the boys who were getting things ready.

The boys looked to both be in their early 20s. They were both strikingly handsome. Just as dirty and smelly looking as Jack, just handsome.

They paid literally no attention to Kelly. They went about their jobs like robots. Kelly thought maybe she should have bought a colada for the boys but she was running late. They could use some coffee she thought.

At around 6:20 am they were on their way. Out past the reef and moving along at around 15 knots. The journey to find her father in Cuba had officially begun.

Kelly had been thinking about her Dad a lot over the last 24 hours. How much he meant to her and how much she loved him.

When he died she took it very hard. Like most people. She was a Daddy's little girl. They did most things together and were pretty much inseparable. Kelly loved her Daddy very much. And now. Well, now, he might actually be alive and not dead.

Living in Cuba no less and who knows maybe he's remarried and even may have kids. What would she say to them? She wondered if they knew. Did they know he had a left a whole family behind?

The ocean was so calm and pretty this morning as the sun come up. It was peaceful. It was like it was just the four of them out there. The rest of the world was somewhere else. Somewhere else not as beautiful.

It was going to take a few hours to get from Key West to Cuba. 84 nautical miles to Havana. This time of day was the prettiest.

Kelly used the time to think about what she was going to say to her father. What was going to happen? She thought about how excited she was going to be when she saw him. She also thought about what on earth he was thinking with all of this. Not really dead. How did he even pull that off?

She also thought of the possibility that Jack truly was a moron. What if this person he says is her Dad, isn't? Jack is after all a drunk. And a bit of an idiot. He's old, maybe senile. Could this all be for nothing? Could Kelly make this trip for no reason at all, other than a ride to Cuba? What happens when they got to Cuba? What then?

Kelly was riddled with anxiety.

CHAPTER 11

Whiskey Sours.

RONNIE WAS STILL FULL OF GUILT. He hadn't talked to Kelly at all yesterday. After she left his apartment, Ronnie drank, a bunch, and then took a nap. By the time he woke up it was late. He wanted to call Kelly but figured at this point it would just be better to wait till tomorrow.

Now tomorrow is here. Today.

He reached for his cell and hit Kelly's picture which dialed her number.

It rang 4 or 5 times and went to voicemail.

"Hey Kel, it's me. I wanted to talk to you today about what happened with us. Please gimme a call when you get this. I'm really sorry. You can even text me if you want. Alright, bye."

He wondered why the hell he mentioned texting. Ronnie hated texting. As a writer the thought of also communicating with people by writing annoyed him.

It's like the idea of working for a greasy burger joint and then coming home to make a burger, he thought.

Anyway, there it was. A call. An apology even. What could she possibly want other than that.

He had done his part. He didn't really want to put that much more effort into the whole thing. Quite honestly, he'd rather she didn't call back. Let this rest for the day now and they could talk tomorrow. Ronnie was a bit of a slow mover.

He stared at his cell. Waiting for it to ring. Looking at the time on the top of the phone. The percentage of battery, 78%. How the fuck is it at 78%

when he just unplugged it an hour ago?

Ronnie had owned every generation of iPhone since the second one. He was now on the 7th version. He was an iPhone guy, but the batteries sucked!

He started to think about yesterday. The shit that Kelly laid on him about her Dad. Some heavy shit. He winced when he thought of his response. He had to go get her. He had to make this right.

He got dressed and hopped on his own scooter and headed to Dan's where he figured she would be.

It was after Noon. She might be hanging out there. Or maybe she pulled a day shift.

When he arrived at Dan's and slid into the gravel parking lot, he didn't notice Kelly's scooter anywhere. It was an obvious Key West scooter. She had just short of a million bumper stickers all over the goddamn thing.

Jorge was behind the bar, and outside of one lone old man at one of the picnic tables, Ronnie was it.

Ronnie didn't know Jorge that well. Had seen him around, but never really took the time to get to meet him. He never really took the time to meet anyone.

"Hey, Jorge. How's it going?"

"What's up?" Jorge just looked up quickly. Not really giving a shit that Ronnie was standing right in front of him.

"I was looking for Kelly? Is she working today?"

"I don't know man. Heard she left town."

Ronnie took a small step back, a kind of roll of his heels.

"Left town? Are you shitting me?"

"Heard she went to Cuba with Jack."

"Jack?! The asshole from here?"

Ronnie instantly regretted calling him an asshole. He remembered that Jorge and Jack were pals.

"Hey man, I happened to like that asshole!"

"I know man, I'm sorry. I'm just shocked that she went to Cuba with him."

It was the second time Ronnie said he was sorry in the last 10 minutes. He didn't like it. Not one damn bit.

"What's there to be shocked about, man? There's nobody better to hitch a ride with then Captain Jack."

Right, Ronnie thought. How about the fucking captain from the Titanic?

"Do you know when they left or any of the details?"

"Yea, they left this morning. A few hours ago. The captain swung by my house before he left and asked if I wanted go. I told him I couldn't cause I was working today. "

Ronnie had a million questions for Jorge but couldn't think of one of them. His mind was racing.

CHAPTER 12

Horacio.

THEY HAD BEEN ON THE BOAT for around 2 hours. Better than half way there. Half way to Cuba. Kelly was really starting to get excited. It reminded her of fishing on the other side of the reef when she was a kid. She spent a lot of hours out past the reef with her Dad.

Of course the only difference was she hadn't been out on the water in over 20 years. She had land legs and a land stomach. After all that throwing up at Ronnie's the other day, her stomach and back muscles still hurt and her throat was still sore.

All that was a problem, because like many times before, the Florida straits were starting to get a little rough. And Kelly was starting to feel it.

The Florida Straits was dangerous. She often thought about Cuban refugees who made that journey on a regular basis on rafts. Rafts!! Sometimes no more than a 6 person raft with twice that many people on it. That was scary.

As she was thinking about those refugees, the wind really started to pick up. The chill in the air was noticeable. Whenever you feel a chill in the air on a hot summer day, nine times out of ten a storm is coming.

The wind made Kelly shiver. There was nothing to her. Just skin and bone. She may have weighed 130 pounds. And that's after a big meal. She was tiny. Her mother was too.

The wind picked up even more and now the sky turned a dark gray. The clouds, big ominous clouds, rolled their way. Or THEY rolled into the clouds. It was hard to tell.

Jack and his crew noticed right away that shit was about to hit the fan. They immediately jumped into action and got ready. They had all seen this kind of weather too many times to count. They knew it was going south real quick.

Jack told Kelly to go below. "You better head down, Missy. It's about to start blowing!!"

There was no way Kelly was going below. She needed to stay right where she was. If she went down below the chances of getting sick at least doubled. She needed air and she needed the sides of the boat. Needed to be near the sides of the boat. Especially if all hell was about to break.

"I gotta stay where there's air!"

"Suit yourself. Put your life jacket on and find something heavy to hold on to!!"

Jack was screaming. He had too. Kelly was surprised he had that strong of a voice. But this was Jack's element. This is where he'd spent most of his adult life. This was his wheelhouse.

Kelly scrambled to find her life jacket. It was hard making her way to it because the boat was really starting to pitch. The winds were real strong now.

"We're going right into her boys!! Get ready!!" Jack yelled to the brothers. "Whoooo!! I love this weather!!!" Jack screamed to no one in particular. He was loving this. Kelly on the other hand was not. She was scared.

The rain began to fall. First huge drops and then the sky just opened up like somebody stuck the clouds with a huge pin and they just bust wide open like a water balloon.

The sky at this point was almost completely black. The boat was pitching hard back and forth. If she had to guess, and she didn't spend a lot of time looking, but these looked like 20-foot waves.

This is it, Kelly thought. This is how I'm going to die. Out here in the middle of an ocean. End up getting eaten by sharks. Just great.

About to find out shit she never knew about her dad and then never even making it out there. All of this because of her lying asshole father. She all of a sudden was so fucking mad at him.

"You MOTHERFUCKER, DAD!! You see what you're putting me through!!"

The boat would tilt now almost completely to one side. A good wave in the right spot and this baby would be taking on water. Quick. And once this kind of boat starts to take on water, it wouldn't be long before it was on the ocean floor.

Jack was moving as fast as he could. Putting all of his remaining strength into trying to control the boat. It was a losing battle. The waves continued to pound the sides of the boat. Crashing up over the boat now. This was bad.

Terrifying.

Kelly was trying to hang on with every ounce of strength she had. It became harder and harder to do with every huge wave. All of a sudden one of the boys, who ended up just too close to the side, was swept away as a wave crashed over. In an instant he was gone. In the panic of the moment it was hard to tell for sure if he was overboard.

Jack knew. He saw it. He was really struggling at this point just to stay with the boat. But he was an old man. With not much strength.

He was doing the best he could.

Within what seemed like seconds, the second crewmember was gone as well. Washed over to now join his brother. As Kelly looked out she saw two dots in the water for just a second and then they were ... just gone.

There was no possible way to save them. In much better circumstances it would have been extremely difficult. In these circumstances, there was just no way.

So now it's just Kelly and Jack.

Kelly is no help at all. All she's doing is hanging on for dear life. But everything is so wet, her hands and everything she was trying to hold onto. The floor of the boat was difficult to keep your footing. She was sliding from side to side and she just wasn't sure how much longer she could hold on.

Just then, the biggest wave yet, it had to be 20 feet high, slammed into the side of the boat. Jack was just in the wrong place at the wrong time. Kelly watched as the tired old man went flying over the side as the wave receded.

He was gone.

Kelly was now more terrified than ever.

She was left alone to fight this storm.

She realized it was a losing fight. All she had to do was stay on the boat and stay alive. That was it. And that was a tall order.

The storm raged on for what seemed like hours but in reality was maybe 20 minutes. Kelly had managed to get down on the wet floor and hold onto some tie downs. She continued to think she couldn't hold on much longer and how much longer is the fucking storm going to last??

All she could do was watch and wait. And pray.

She never prayed to God so much as right now. She begged God for protection and to get her through this. As you're in this position and facing certain death, she realized it's not so much your life flashing before your eyes, it's more like memories that pop into your head.

There she was at her 6th birthday party.

And at her first communion
Her first day of school
When she got her tonsils out
First day of high school and then graduation.
All of it.
Popping in and popping out.

She was starting to lose consciousness. She knew she couldn't lose because then she wouldn't be able to hang on any longer.

But at some point, with this incredible storm raging all around her, it seemed futile. It seemed like there was no possible way out of this. 3 men on the boat just died, what was so special about her that she would survive.

It was the end for Kelly. She was sure of it.

And then ... darkness. She was out.

It was a little bizarre because even though she blacked out she could still feel the rain and wind hitting her. She could still feel herself hanging on for dear life. She knew she was being tossed back and forth.

She felt the wet. All over her. At some point, at some level, you can't get any wetter. When you're soaked through to your bones, that's it. Kelly was soaked through to her bones.

She felt all of this and consciously was aware of it all.

How much longer can this possibly go on? She remembered thinking that.

Then total darkness.
Total blackness
No more memories
No more feeling wet or hearing the waves. It was silent. Dead silent. There were no more thoughts or feelings, just darkness.

After more than hour of this storm battering this

small boat, it was over. Just like that. Just a little bit of rain, but blue skies on the horizon.

Thank God. It was over.

The normal sounds of the ocean. The normal sounds of the boat rocking and creaking.

And then feelings. Thoughts.

Very slowly.

The loud creak of the wood floors first and then the sound of the water.

Then thoughts.

Am I still on the boat?

Am I alive?

Where am I anyway? Why would I be on a boat?

Slowly her thoughts and memories came back. She could feel her fingers and toes come alive and she could hear herself breathing.

She very slowly opened her eyes.

She was alive.

She beat the storm.

She beat the storm!!!

She was elated to be alive but was still moving very slowly. She stayed on the floor of the boat. Swaying back and forth. She started to think about what just happened in the last hour.

Those handsome boys she was certain were gone. She thought about their mothers back in Key West who maybe had a feeling that something was wrong with their sons. Moms feel that kind of thing sometimes.

Kelly felt all at once a strong urge to stand. She felt like at that moment if she didn't stand she was going to die. She never felt closer to death than right now. It was almost panic. Here she had made it through this hurricane but now in the calm, eerie silence afterwards, she felt close to death.

She knew she had to move. Now!

She very slowly started to gather herself and feel her legs move and get up under her. Her arms moved and her fingers and hands. Everything started to move. She was like an old car coming back to life. Her engine was turning over and over and over but it just wasn't firing yet.

After several minutes of trying she was now on her knees and seeing blue sky for the first time since the storm. She immediately thanked God.

She wasn't a religious woman but at that moment she felt saved. She felt there had to be some force that kept her from being washed over the side like 3 of her shipmates were.

Before long, she was on her feet. Slowly. Very wobbly.

But she was up.

She took a step and then another and then another.

The sea was flat calm and she was just sailing along. Floating.

There was a lot of damage on the boat but she was still floating.

She knew she wasn't dead but didn't feel quite alive either.

Holy shit!

She was so grateful to be alive. All of a sudden though, it dawned on her that everyone else that she got on the boat with in Key West was DEAD!

She was by herself.

She didn't know anything about getting a boat where you wanted it to go. The panic that set in now was far worse than during the middle of the storm. She was truly all alone. She didn't know where she was or how far from Cuba she was or if she was even heading in the right direction.

The water was at this point almost flat calm. The

silence was deafening. Just a slight sound of the water gently slapping into the side of the boat. The engines were down. She was floating to ... wherever. Wherever the water took her. On some level it was incredibly freeing. She could end up in the Bahamas or Costa Rica or Haiti. Could indeed end up anywhere BUT Cuba.

On the other hand, it was the most incredibly terrifying feeling she'd ever had in her life.

Good thing about Jack, he was a crusty old captain and he knew how to prepare a boat for a trip. There was plenty of water and food to last at least a week, more if she could parcel it out.

She was actually afraid to drink any of the water or eat any of the food because she was afraid of running out.

That was crazy of course. There was plenty ... for now anyway.

Kelly heard lots of critters in the ocean too. Some of them sounded big and scary. Whenever she heard a noise from the ocean she would scurry to the other side of the boat.

After what seemed like hours and hours but was actually more like 45 minutes, she relented and opened her first bottle of water. There was a case left. Plenty!

The water, even though a tad on the warm side, was delicious and incredibly refreshing. It was like the first bottle of water she'd ever had.

She drank fast at first and then, half way through, much much slower. She made the rest of the bottle last quite awhile.

The sun was beating down on her. It felt just a few feet above her. Unrelenting. Not a cloud in the sky.

No respite

Just sun.

Harsh and
Hot
Unforgiving

The sun could've cared less that she was on this disabled boat in the Florida Straits. Didn't care that her boat wasn't running and that she didn't know where she was going. Didn't care one bit. All the sun cared about was being the sun. Sunny.

That was its job.

Kelly had now been out here one full day and night.

24 hours.

It still all looked the same. That's the thing about the ocean. It sure doesn't change much.

When Kelly woke on the start of her second day in ocean jail, she saw something in the distance. It was rather large and seemed to be floating towards her.

She couldn't make out what it was. Probably some kind of dead fish or something. Or maybe a square grouper.

Back in the 1970's in Key West drugs would often float into shore. They would be these big bales of marijuana. They would just float in. They had been pushed off drug boats making their way to America from points south. When the coast guard would intercede, the drug boats who saw the coast guard coming would push as much pot as they could off the side of the boat.

The bales would float. Like a big fish. Like a grouper. And of course a bale is ... square.

Hence, square grouper.

So maybe that's what this was. It would be a good size one if it was.

It got closer and closer and she still couldn't make it out. A dead fish. Yes, most likely.

It got even closer.

When it was about 20 feet away she could make it

out a little better but didn't believe her eyes.

She'd been out here in the sun too long.

It looked like ... a

Person!

And no person that was alive could float like that.

She got scared. Not only to confirm that it was a person but to have to see it up close.

As the object floated right up to the side of the boat, Kelly screamed. And it wasn't just a little yelp or yip ... it was a loud almost blood curdling scream.

It was a dead body.

It was floating face down and was missing huge chunks of itself. Fish. Or sharks. They were sampling the body buffet. By the looks of it, they weren't crazy about this particular buffet. There wasn't that much missing.

She very slowly grabbed the pole next to her. And for whatever reason, she never really knew why, she ...

Poked it.

Did she think it would roll over and say "HI! My name's Bob. How do you do?"

She wasn't sure. She poked it again.

It did a full roll and turned to face her. For the second time in less than 5 minutes, she screamed! Much much harder than the first time.

It was the kind of scream that you couldn't make up.

This was the kind of scream that came from inside your soul, from deep within and built and built all in the fraction of a nano second and came bursting out.

It was pure terror.

She recognized this floating human grouper.

She recognized him very well.

He didn't look so good, of course he never really did. Not as long as she'd known him.

It was dirty, old Jack!

He'd been washed away and there was no way that a man in his shape at his age could possibly fight that storm. Even the two able bodied brothers who were in their 20's and were strapping young guys couldn't have fought that storm for long ... of course longer than Jack could.

But there he was. His face really hadn't changed much.

That wasn't a part of the buffet.

He looked more peaceful than she'd ever seen him. No more scowl, which was so much a part of the way he looked every day you wouldn't notice him any other way.

Now Jack was fascinated by things that were waterproof and things that floated. His whole life.

When the technology created things that were and could do both, it blew his fucking mind.

Kelly remembers the day that Jack came into the bar with his new purchase. He couldn't stop showing it off.

It was a brand new, bright red, waterproof, floatable wallet.

Man, he thought that was just so cool.

He had Kelly fetch a pitcher full of water so he could demonstrate the effectiveness of his new purchase.

She of course did. She'd never seen Jack so excited. Course, it didn't take much. Jack had so little in his life to look forward to, a new floating wallet was a big damn deal.

It was funny.

One of the few times Jack was ever funny. He demonstrated that wallet over and over again. Pushing it further and further down until the water in the pitcher overflowed.

He'd make this funny wide-eyed look on his face that just cracked everyone up. Those were good times, not just at the bar, but in Kelly's life in general.

She was just starting to get her life together. It was

soon after her asshole boyfriend got all chopped up.

Funny how something like a memory of a day where someone showed how they could keep their money dry under water, could take you back to that point of your life.

So fast forward to today. This awful situation that Kelly found herself in. (Of course, seeing Jack, it could've been much much worse)

Here's old asshole drunk Jack now floating, dead, in the ocean. Probably exactly where he'd want to die.

And sure as shit, floating not far from him was his wallet.

Bright red.

Floating

Sonofabitch

It really did float.

Kelly put her hands in the bathtub warm water and moved them in the direction of herself trying to get the wallet to come to mommy.

After about 30 seconds it was within reach.

She had it.

It was in her hand now.

She sat back hard with the red wallet in her hand. It was sealed pretty good and when Kelly pried it open, it was like Geraldo prying open Capone's vault.

She first, of course, checked inside for cash. Much to her surprise there was actually a pretty big pile of cash in there. Maybe a thousand or more dollars.

Alright Jack.

Thanks buddy.

She flipped through the wallet looking at different kinds of ID and different pictures.

It was while looking through the pictures that something hit her. She recognized the people in these pictures. All of them. It was her family. Her Dad and grandparents. Cousins and nephews and nieces.

Then she stumbled onto a very handsome picture of her Dad siting next to Uncle Joe. She pulled the picture out and stared at it for some time. Really looking hard. Dad was so handsome. He must've been maybe 30 in this picture. Her Uncle Joe was a nice looking man also.

It was so strange to her as to why Jack had a picture of her Dad and Uncle in his wallet. She flipped the picture over like most people do. Sometimes people write shit on the back of old pictures.

On the back it said, "Me and brother, Frank"

Now it was even more strange. This clearly was a picture owned by her Uncle Joe. Why?

Wait just a second!

Could it?

No!

She looked through more pictures in the wallet. More of her family. There were maybe 10 pictures in there ... all of Kelly's family.

Then she hadn't even looked at it yet, Jacks ID. His driver's license. It was a bad picture of Jack ... there wasn't many good ones.

Kelly stared at the ID for a long time. A LONG time.

Especially one line on Jacks license.

She couldn't pull her eye off that one line and by the way she couldn't shut her mouth.

It was wide open.

The line she was staring at said:

JOSEPH ANTHONY ALVAREZ

Jack WAS her Uncle Joe.

Holy. Fucking. Shit.

CHAPTER 13

Big Bro.

FRANKIE WAS STUNNED. He just found out he had a big brother he never knew about. And now he was here. His big brother George. Frankie always just thought it was him and Joe.

George sat and looked at Frankie for a little bit watching his reaction. His face. George was trying to read Frankie's face. No luck. He couldn't quite figure out what Frankie was feeling. Happy? Sad? Pissed off? Confused? What??

Finally after what seemed like a year and a half, Frankie closed his mouth. Stop just gawking at his brother. Then, Frankie spoke, "You're my brother?" Three words? Really? After all that silence, 3 words?

"Yes, I am your older brother."

That phrase sat in the air above Frankie's head for a moment. It just hung there. Frankie at 18 years old just couldn't grasp this. He did the only thing he could do.

He started to cry.

Slow at first, but then sobbing. Right there at the DQ.

His big brother reached over and put his hand over Frankie's.

To think that Frankie's whole childhood would have been likely different if he had a big brother in it. All of the things in Frankie's life that might have been tough or tricky, things he sure couldn't talk about with his Dad or his little brother about, he might've been able to with a big brother. Lots of Frankie's friends had big brothers.

He always thought it would be cool. Someone that always had his back. Was always there for him. It would have been nice to have a big brother.

And now, at 18, here he was.

Coming back now. For what reason? To take Frankie away with him to some big city. He sure didn't want that.

"Listen, Frankie, don't cry buddy. I'm sorry. I really am. This wasn't my call. Mom and Dad thought it was best. I was a smart-ass kid with a shitty attitude. We lived in a small town, cut off from the world, you know how it is, everyone knows everyone's business. To have a kid that was this much trouble ... man that was a problem."

Frankie was drying his eyes off now. He started to understand a little bit now.

"Plus, ya know, Mom and Dad were young. Real young. I mean the thing of it is they weren't even married yet."

NOW it made sense.

An unplanned pregnancy with two teenagers on a tiny island. Oh yea, Frankie could certainly understand how that could be a problem.

"So they sent me north. I went to this home where there were other kids my age that gave their parents a bunch of shit or maybe they were in the same situation as me. That kind of thing happened. Still happens."

Frankie was trying to do the math. He knew his parents were a little bit older than his friends' parents. He just figured they got a late start.

"How old ARE you, George?"

"28."

Frankie had an older brother that was 10 years older than him! He knew his dad was 44 years old. So that meant he was 15 when George was born. 15-year-old boys didn't become fathers in those days. Maybe not now either. Frankie started to see what a scandal this really was. Then he thought about his mom, who is 43.

She gave birth at 14, pregnant at probably 13 or going on 14.

That WAS a big deal. And to think on top of it all, the kid they do have turns out to be an asshole that no one in town has anything good to say about. Not just an asshole, but an asshole bastard. They were probably relieved to get rid of him.

They tried. They gave it the ol college try. It just didn't work out. Neither Frank nor Charlotte had the tools or skills to make it all work.

What amazes Frankie is that he just didn't know. He never knew and what's worse no one ever thought to tell him. THIS is how he has to find out? A stranger comes to town, takes him out and sits him down at a restaurant, and a shitty one at that, and tells him the whole story? Really?

"Ok, so now what?" Frankie was getting over the tears pretty quickly.

"I knew you were now old enough to know and I thought I had a great opportunity for you," said his big brother.

"An 18 year old man can go and do things that a 30 year old man with a record can't."

"So that's it? It's about doing something for you. It's about what can I do for you? You come down here after all this time and then WANT something from me?"

George could tell this whole thing was going south. If there was one thing George was good at, it was talking. Convincing people of what he feels is right. Or wrong. He had the gift of the gab, as they say.

"Lookit, Frankie, all I'm telling you is I have a chance for you to make a lot of money. And who knows, maybe even more than I think. And maybe somewhere inside me this is my chance of saying I'm sorry. Ya know? I'm sorry for missing your life. Not being there for you when you needed me."

Frankie liked George from the moment he met him. Sensed something in him. Not a goodness so much, Frankie didn't sense that George was necessarily a good man.

He just thought he had something that Frankie needed. Not just a brother, but a chance at something bigger.

A chance for Frankie to have a shot. A real shot. No matter how hard he worked at school or the baseball team or at his Dads garage, he'd always be here. Right here. In Key West. In this tiny little town that was just a dot in the ocean. What chance did Frankie really have?

What really were Frankie's chances? Choices?

George represented something bigger. From the moment Frankie laid eyes on George, he seemed bigger. He seemed like he was different.

No one in Key West had a suit like that. Or a car like that. Or talked like that. It was different. And even before Frankie realized that George was his brother, he felt like there was a chance there. Somehow. Something different.

"Ok, so … what? What's the offer? What is it you want me to do? How am I gonna make all this money you keep talking about?"

"I want you to go to Cuba. There's a job there for you. A big job. You speak any Spanish?"

Frankie spoke Spanish very well actually.

"Yea, a little."

George looked back at him and smiled, "Perfect. Just perfect!"

CHAPTER 14

Kelly Was Out There.

AS RONNIE PULLED OUT of Dan's parking lot and back onto the main drag all he could think about was Kelly on a goddamn boat with that old crusty fuck, floating across an ocean on her way to Cuba and into god knows what kind of trouble.

This was the action of a girl who did things without thinking them through. A girl who wasn't too bright. A woman who would do something rash.

The very thought of doing what she's doing not only pissed Ronnie off but it terrified him.

And there it was. Maybe that's what this whole thing was. Fear.

Fear of the unknown. Fear of finding out the truth. Of finding out the news, whether it be good or bad or even just awful, but finding out anyway.

Ronnie had carved out a nice life for himself, not just here and now on this little island, but in general. He was comfortable. Not just financially but he was in the zone. His zone. His little bubble. He did nothing he didn't want to do. He'd been blessed with a talent to write. To be creative. To make a lot of money doing something he generally liked.

Because of that, what Kelly was doing right now made zero sense to him. It would probably never make sense to him.

Chasing after the unknown. Chasing after some dream that vanished a long time ago. A dream that you woke up from a long long time ago. A dream that could very well be a nightmare.

No guy, by the way, likes the pop-in. He's home,

minding his own business, sitting in his underwear, watching TV, and all of a sudden there's a knock on the door. He freezes. Who the fuck is knocking on my door? If I mute the TV and stay real still, they'll just go away.

That's how most guys are.

No guy liked the pop-in, and now Kelly was crossing an ocean to pop-in on her father who she thought was dead. A father she thought she lost years ago. A father she obviously didn't know. And a father that clearly didn't want to know her either.

Yes. This was a great idea, Kelly. Great. This couldn't possibly go wrong. And then on top of it you're on a boat with a 100 year old Fucking drunk crossing an ocean??

Oh yes indeed. This is a can't miss. You're going to just nail this one, Ronnie thought.

Either way, as angry with Kelly as he was, he found himself a little worried. No, more than a little worried. He was still shocked that she even went. Ronnie thought what would be best was just going home, turning on the TV, grabbing his favorite glass, and pouring some of the whiskey sour mix that was already mixed in his fridge into that glass and relax. Maybe noodle this a little more and see what he should do next.

When he got home his dogs were of course waiting for him. Their reaction was the same if he came home from checking the mail or a trip to Europe. They were going nuts.

They jumped and jumped on him.

Every once in a while the smaller dog would scratch Ronnie's leg and he would yell out scaring the shit out of both of them.

He turned the TV on first. That was sort of habit. Unless Ronnie was writing, or had an idea or concept, the TV would be on. Sometimes even muted, but on. Ronnie found it comforting. Almost as if someone was in the room with him.

Ronnie muted the TV before the picture was even visible.

He walked into the kitchen, grabbed his glass, got 2 ice cubes and poured the mix over the ice. Perfect.

He walked back into the living room. And what he saw on the TV made him stumble backwards about a half a step before the wall caught him.

The TV was on CNN and the news wasn't good. They had the resident weatherman, Richard VonFuckFace on talking about the hurricane that was swirling in the Atlantic currently. Shit! That's right. It IS hurricane season after all.

And it was a big storm. Bearing down. And it was right in between Cuba and Key West. Right were Kelly might be. He set his glass down on the wooden coffee table and plunked down hard in his leather lazy-boy.

He was shocked at this development. Shocked to think Kelly could be in that mess.

As it turns out and as Ronnie was starting to realize, he had stronger feelings for Kelly than he'd ever let on. Ronnie was terrible at relationships but great at sex. For the last several years Kelly was just Sex.

Had he developed feelings that until just now he's realized? Did he love Kelly? Well he was worried about her. He did feel something in his stomach when he thought of her.

Maybe he was in love with her.

Christ! How did that happen?? Ronnie had paid very close attention to this matter and was very careful NOT to fall in love with Kelly.

But now as he sat and watched this storm swirling, still with no volume, he thought maybe he did love her. Maybe he did.

Honestly it felt nice to Ronnie to think that maybe he was in love. Truth is it sucked to be alone. Ronnie just got used to it.

It was nice to have a girls touch around the apartment. Kelly always brought fresh flowers when she came by. She always had a bright disposition and opened the curtains. She cleaned more than what you would clean with a broom and vacuum. She cleaned Ronnie's heart.

He didn't know what that meant. It's what he was thinking.

Everything ended on a bad note too.

She stormed out and peeled off.

Shit!

What the fuck could he do now?

Kelly was out there. In the middle of the ocean. With an old drunk asshole. In a hurricane.

Fuck!!

CHAPTER 15

Shark Shit.

SO NOW WHAT? What's Kelly supposed to do now. She's in a beat up, battered sail boat with no sails and busted up engine, sailing gods knows which direction, all by herself with no help and now, NOW, her dead uncle floating along with her.

He couldn't have been dead long. Couldn't have been in the water long.

But it didn't take long for that skinny little body to attract attention out there in the ocean.

As Kelly was staring off at the horizon, hoping and dreaming to see land, so engrossed, she never even saw them.

They were good size too. Hard to miss if you were paying attention. She wasn't.

This wasn't going to take long and it sure wasn't going to be pretty.

The hammerhead sharks, at least 3 of them, were probably 8 or 9 feet long, circling and circling, until they were sure what they were smelling was what they wanted. Sure that there would be nothing to stop them.

And then, STRIKE!!

One shark bit first and the other two grabbed on and it was off to the races. Poor dead Uncle Joe didn't stand a chance. He was about to die again.

Kelly all at once noticed and screamed. First out of fear and then anger.

"You fuckers!!!"

She grabbed a nearby oar and starting swinging. So wildly she was sure she hit Joe a few times.

"Get out of here!!"

It was futile.

Much much too little and way too late.

It was a feeding frenzy. Joe was ripped into little pieces and swallowed. Kelly was shocked to see so much blood and lots and lots of other squirty things that come out of a human body when it's being torn apart by a shark.

For a brief moment Kelly found herself thinking it would've been way better getting shot in front of that courthouse in Miami. Way better.

There was absolutely nothing she could do. She threw the oar down and started to cry. She started to think about Ronnie. How much she loved him and how much she wished he was here now. Holding her. Telling her it was ok. Telling her what to do next.

Ronnie would know. He was such a smart man.

Kelly plunked down, kicked the oar out of the way and cried. A good cry. One of those cries where you feel so much better afterwards.

She took a peek over the side and there was zero sign of Uncle Joe. None. A couple articles of clothing and a puddle or two of blood and lots of DNA.

In just a few short hours, her long lost thought to be dead Uncle Joe would be shark shit.

Great. Just great!

Now what? The only man who may have known where her dad was and the only one who could've gotten to him in Cuba was now being digested by some hammerhead sharks.

Well, actually, they were still licking their lips so to speak. He wouldn't get digested for another hour or two.

This thought made Kelly chuckle a little bit.

So now, truly, Kelly is alone. As far as people anyway. God knows what else is in that ocean circling the boat like water vultures. Waiting for her to give up or slip.

She really was getting scared. The ocean is just so daunting. So big. As far as the eye could see there was just nothing. Water. She wondered how much water. Like, how many gallons. Millions? Billions? Trillions?

What comes after trillions? She thought.

Kelly felt herself getting tired. And hot. Her face and the back of her neck felt as if they were on fire. They were hot to the touch.

There was still plenty of water on the boat. Way more than she thought she would ever need.

She decided to go below and get out of the sun. Maybe just lay down for a minute or two. She had been through an awful lot in the last 24 hours. She started to think she was tougher than she knew.

Her mind drifted back to Ronnie. She loved him so much and wished he was here with her. She knew Ronnie hated the water and boats and anyone else who enjoyed water or boats. He'd have no clue what to do in this situation, but at least he could comfort her. Hold her. Tell her it wouldn't be much longer.

Anything.

There was a tiny little filthy bed down below that looked as if 32 dirty old pirates slept there before her. She figured at this point she was probably just as filthy and stinky as any of them.

She sat on the bed.

For the first time since she left Key West on this God forsaken journey she stopped.

She thought. Thought about what a bad idea this trip was. How impulsive it was. How crazy! What did she hope to accomplish? To meet her father? To see him again? A man who abandoned his family years ago. A man who clearly didn't give a shit about her. Why did she care so much about him?

Maybe closure. Maybe so she could see him again and tell him to fuck off. Tell him something she wasn't able to do years ago to tell him goodbye. And then what? Hop on a boat and float back to Key West?

Just a crazy idea. All of it.

But, on the bright side, she'll always be able to tell people she rode out a hurricane in the Atlantic Ocean.

That is if she ever actually sees people again.

She decided to lay back a little on the garbage heap that was this mattress.

All she heard was the ocean saying hello and then goodbye on the side of the boat. Back and forth. Back and forth.

It was almost like a rocking chair.

She could feel her eyes becoming heavy.

And then. Sleep came.

Kelly slept hard.

She dreamed about the whole situation.

Actually she dreamed about the part of the story where her and Ronnie meet up with her Dad. And he's just as handsome as she remembered. At least in her eyes. He was so happy to see her.

He was smiling. Reached out his arms to hug her. Ronnie walking right next to her. All of her fears and hesitation and anger were gone. There, in her dream, was Daddy. She was so close to him she could smell his old spice.

His teeth were white. His jet black hair was messed up, (which it never was when she was a kid. It was always on point)

She got within 10 feet of him, in her dream, and then his face changed. His look went from happy to horror in one second flat. It was such a look of horror it scared the shit out of Kelly. He was waving. At someone? At her?

He started to scream something. Everything was

moving so slow. She saw every emotion. Every expression.

Then, just like that, it was normal speed again.

"Kelly for Christsake get down!!!!"

Her father was screaming at her to get down. She didn't understand. But instinct was a good thing and she got down.

She looked up from the ground just as the first bullets pierced his shirt. It was as if it was a scene in some movie. She felt like she could see every bullet enter his body.

One after another after another after another. It felt like an eternity. And the bullets were still coming. Now she saw red. All over his white guayabera shirt. He stumbled forward and then backward. He kept going back further and further. Until he was down.

"NOOOOO!" Kelly screamed! It was the loudest hardest scream of her life.

"DADDY!!!"

He didn't move. He was covered now in blood. One man walked forward with his hands down, a gun in his right hand, down by his side, walking. Closer and closer to her dad.

Until he was right on top of her slightly groaning father. He was still alive. Barely, but yes.

Then the tall man, very thin, very ugly, pointed the gun straight down, right over her Dad's head and pulled the trigger. She had never seen anyone shot in the head. Not in real life. In the movies it was always very dramatic and explosive.

But here? Now? There was a single pop. Like a cap gun. Her father made a reflexive jump and blood flowed quickly and thickly out of his head.

Not explosive at all.

Just a pop and blood.

A lot of blood.

The man kept walking in the same direction. Very matter of factly. Never turned around. And after about 20 paces he let the gun fall from his gloved hand. She watched him for a long while before looking back at the ground where her father continued to bleed. A lot!

Then another bang. Different this time. And again. And again. BANG! BANG!

Where was that coming from?

BANG!

All at once Kelly woke up. Woke up crying. It was so real. She looked around. She instantly noticed just how badly that mattress smelled.

And then, it all came back to her. Where she was and what she was doing. And the BANG! Was still there. Still banging.

She wiped the tears out of her eyes, fixed her hair and went to investigate the noise.

CHAPTER 16

Logistics.

"HERE'S THE THING, FRANKIE," George was looking Frankie dead in the eye.

"A lot of shit happens in the ocean between Key West and Cuba. Shit no one knows about. A guy like you can make a lot of money bringing things to Cuba."

Frankie didn't have to think very long for his next question, "what kind of things?"

"C'mon Frankie. I shouldn't have to say it. You're a big boy."

"Drugs?? Are you asking me to carry drugs from Key West to Cuba?? Is that what this about?? You're out of your damn mind!"

George sat back hard on his side of the booth.

"Wait a minute, Frankie. I didn't say that!"

"But it's what you meant. Isn't it?"

All of a sudden George's cards were starting to show. He didn't want to flip over his whole hand yet, but it was close. He knew it was like feeding a squirrel for the first time. You don't run up to it flailing your arms, you move very slowly and carefully. And that's what George was trying to do with Frankie.

"Frankie, listen, I need a man in Cuba. I need a man that can go in there and make money ... for both of us. They know me there. I'm not welcome in Cuba."

"So how does it work? I just go there and then what?"

Frankie was starting to feel like this might not be a bad idea after all. Maybe there was something to this idea. Maybe he could make a lot of money.

"I have a place there. It's nothing great. But it's

clean and there's AC. We get you over there and get you set up. The place is in the middle of Havana. Once we get you set up the word goes out that this new guy in town can get shit. Whatever you need ... pain pills, coke, pot and even heroin. When the rest of the world comes to town on vacation, we get em! Hook em!"

"So we're not pushing this shit on Cubans?"

"Fuck no! They don't have any money to buy our shit. We prey on the tourists that come into Cuba. More and more every year are coming in. We hook em, give a little kick back to Fidel and we're up and running!"

Frankie sat back and closed his eyes. Live on another island. Make a shit load of money. Screw people visiting not his blood. He sat with his eyes closed for quite a while. He tried real hard to think of all the things that could go wrong. Right now, maybe it was George. Maybe it was Frankie being bored with Key West. He wasn't sure. But everything George was saying was really starting to make sense.

"Well, how does this whole thing happen?"

George looked at Frankie. One corner of George's mouth curled up in a tiny little smirk.

"Let's talk logistics, my boy."

CHAPTER 17

Cuba?

THE BANGING WAS AMPLIFIED in Kelly's head. When she got above deck she realized her head was banging more than the noise.

"What the fuck is that noise?!" she muttered to herself. "And, why is that stupid bird flying so damn close to me?"

Then as if struck by lightning, she quickly, a little too quickly maybe, spun around. Birds. Banging.

LAND!!!

Ho-Ly SHIT!!

She had made it!

She had made it!

Kelly was stunned. Here she was. It was a beautiful sunny day and a beautiful thing to see. After all she'd been through she was here!

Well, but where's here?

WAS this Cuba?

She really had no way of knowing for sure. It's not like they had a sign at their beaches that said, Welcome to Cuba, weirdos floating in on a boat.

Kelly didn't really know what to do next. She stumbled and fumbled around the boat for things she would need. She grabbed her bag with all her personal belongings. Paperwork and phone, (yea like that's going to work here.)

She made her way to the side of the boat and looked into the clear water below. She was still a good 50 feet from shore but caught up on a good size rock. There was no other way to get to actual land without getting wet.

She relished the thought of getting wet. But she didn't want her shit getting wet. The bag was supposed to be "waterproof", she thought.

"Well, we're about to find out," she said out loud as with one big heave she threw the bag as far as she could.

It traveled about halfway to shore and lay there. Bobbing right above the surface.

She thought that was pretty good.

The water was maybe 5 feet deep if that, she took one last look and jumped over the side and splashed into that clear warm water.

It was warm. Not refreshing at all. Just wet. She made that goofy walk with her arms parallel to the surface but above water. It was rocky. She walked slowly and gingerly. And carefully. Not much worse than cutting your foot on a rock in the salt water.

She took her time, even though she wanted to race to the beach. Maybe 7 minutes later, she was touching real land. Beach. Some sand. This would be beautiful if she was on vacation, she thought.

She dropped to the ground and just reveled in the stillness of it all. How quiet it was. How sweet the air smelled. The birds flying above and the beautiful sky she had to squint to see. A gentle breeze kissing her on the cheek. This was it.

She knew in her heart she had made the journey through literal hell and this was the paradise known as Cuba.

She fell into sort of a slumber. Closed her eyes and thought what a fucked experience this had been. It might have been 5 minutes or 30, she opened her eyes and a panic attack hit. She had come to the realization of what all of this was.

She thought she was in Cuba. Pretty sure of it. She thought why she was here. The overwhelming feeling of what she had to do, why she came here.

Dad.

CHAPTER 18

Dairy Queen.

SO HERE THEY SAT.

At a Dairy Queen in Key West plotting this wild idea of an international crime ring between Key West, Miami, Chicago and Cuba that would include drugs, merchandise, rum and cigars.

His damn feet were tingling. It felt like he was in space. He couldn't believe this was happening. It felt like a dream.

Could this really be true? Could an 18 year old kid be starting a career with the mafia that could make him millions?

This was just all too much. Too much for anyone to believe, much less an 18 year old kid.

"Alright, so let's keep this simple, kid. All we gotta do is get you down there, which is simple. Once we get you all set up there you'll just stay put. Shit will happen pretty quick. It'll come to you. You're not going to have to do much leg work. Every time an order comes in, you get word to the courier and he relays back home and we make it happen from there."

"How does the stuff get here?"

"That's a good question kid." (Frankie wasn't sure why all of a sudden his big brother was calling him kid, but he didn't mind. Kind of liked it)

"There's boats and planes rolling in and out of that place every day, a few times a day. Mostly planes. We got a partner in the airline and the shipping industry. It all happens pretty quick. You're just the guy in place that puts it all together. You'll keep a list, with no names and no specifics, you'll have to work

81

out some kinda code, then we deliver."

Frankie was truly in disbelief. Who knew this kind of stuff was happening? Certainly not him.

He was really shocked that business was being done this way. It was all news to him.

"All right, so when do we start and how much do I make?" asked Frankie.

"Ah, a true businessman, you're going to do just fine in Cuba." (George pronounced Cuba like Coo-ba)

"The way it works, George continued, "is you get a piece of every item you push. It's 10%. Not much on a bottle of rum, but when you start pushing some coke and heroin and weed, that's going to add up to a lot of scratch."

Frankie was really getting excited about this. Not so much leaving and living in an unknown place, but the idea of money. Having it. And lots of it.

But as he was thinking about all the money, he had a dark thought also. How does he know they'll do what they're saying. How does he know he won't get screwed on the money? And is he going to be protected?

Some solid questions.

That would need answering.

Soon enough.

CHAPTER 19

What Now?

RONNIE WAS STILL WATCHING the picture on TV about this God forsaken hurricane in the Atlantic. He still hasn't turned the volume on. For these kind of pictures you didn't need volume. The images were bad enough.

Hurricanes were no joke. They brought death and destruction wherever they landed. This hurricane was heading towards Key West ... fast.

If Kelly was out there, chances were pretty good she was feeling it. Maybe even hanging on for dear life. It's a thought Ronnie had to shake his head to clear.

Maybe she'd made it in time. Maybe she was past it. Already landing in Cuba. Ronnie had no way of knowing. And maybe that was the worst of it. Not knowing how she was.

It was hard to pin down where Kelly might be in relation to the storm, which they now named Horatio. She could be anywhere in that small boat in the expanse of the Atlantic Ocean.

Christ, what the hell am I going to do now, thought Ronnie.

There's certainly no flights or boats leaving now. He was literally stuck. He couldn't go after her. He wanted to, but knew that was impossible.

He'd have to wait for the storm to pass first.

CHAPTER 20

Good Grief.

KELLY WAS SOAKING WET. And even though it was probably 88 degrees, she was a little cold. The wet clothes and the ocean breeze made her chilly. She was, after all, a Key West girl. Thin blood. Not like those Yankees, anyone north of Key Largo. She called them "thick-bloods".

Kelly wrapped her arms around herself and stood for the first time. She wobbled a little bit, but stood. She thought this must be what they meant when they said, "getting your land legs". Her ocean legs were still keyed up for a rocky boat ride. She stood up and straightened out.

She glanced around this new place she was feeling pretty certain she was in Cuba. She thought what a difference it was coming ashore here rather than Cubans coming ashore in America. She felt like entering this country was the easiest thing in the world.

Just then she heard men talking ... loudly. Their voices were getting closer and louder. She was still squinting and didn't exactly know where they were coming from.

Just heard them getting closer, and louder.

Kelly never had any interest in learning Spanish, even though her whole family spoke it. She never cared. She never thought she'd ever use it. Boy, did she wish she knew it now. Could've been real damn handy!

The men, 3 of them, were on the beach now. She could make out their shadowy silhouettes. She couldn't tell if they sounded angry or friendly.

She wouldn't have to wait too long to find out. They sounded angry!

They approached her much more quickly than she expected. It seemed like just seconds ago they were a mile away.

As she was still sort of staggering up the beach, they were on her. Grabbing her arms and forcing her up the small hill and onto the roadway.

Awaiting them was a small white police vehicle and they roughly shoved her into the back seat.

Up to this point, it was kind of a blur, but now, as reality set in, she was terrified.

Perfect, she thought, I travel across an ocean, during a hurricane, am the only survivor to arrive here in Cuba and within 5 minutes I'm arrested.

It all was happening so fast.

Now they're barreling through the streets of Havana at breakneck speeds towards what she assumed would be a jail.

Good grief!

CHAPTER 21

Jail?

AFTER ABOUT 10 MINUTES, the police car with Kelly in it came to a screeching halt. She didn't speak or read Spanish, but it didn't take a professor to know she was at the jail.

She was roughly taken out of the car and hurried inside. She was cuffed tightly behind her back. When she got inside the jail, there were 3 other Cubans, all speaking very loudly. She assumed they were talking about her. They pointed. They yelled. They grabbed her and pulled her down the hallway. They did it so quickly and roughly, she couldn't catch up. They literally were dragging her down the hall.

When they arrived at the cell, they opened the door and pushed her in. She lost her balance, which she never really had, and fell flat out on her stomach on the filthy floor. The whole place was filthy.

Even the cops were filthy and smelly. There seemed to be a "head" cop or one who seemed to be in charge. He was the meanest out of the bunch. And that was saying something because they were *all* mean.

They slammed the door behind her and left her there. In this dark, filthy, stinky cell. They laughed after the chief made a comment and then walked back up the hallway. The laughter continued as they walked.

There was a sort of bench like thing and she climbed off the ground and sat down on it. Her head was truly spinning. She started to think about the last 24 hours which led her to right here. In a jail. In Cuba.

She was scared. Who wouldn't be? In a foreign country. Not speaking the language. In JAIL! She started to softly cry. She didn't want those cops to know they scared her. Kelly was a conch. She was tough. She'd been through worse than this. Hell, she'd been through worse just getting here. What really scared her now was what are they going to do to her. Are they going to hurt her. Or worse? And what about her father. This was a situation she'd gotten herself into that she certainly never thought of.

CHAPTER 22

It Pays to Know a Jerk.

RONNIE WAS LOST. He felt as bad as he'd ever felt. Sick to his stomach. Wondering and worrying about the woman he'd fallen in love with, without even realizing it. He had thought of every worse case scenario he could. Each time was worse than the one before.

There was no way he could've known that she was alive but in a Cuban jail.

Every scenario running through Ronnie's head had Kelly being killed at sea. A hundred different ways. And it was killing him. He went back to his tree fort apartment to think. There had to be someway he could help her.

Of course this whole time, a pretty fierce hurricane was on its way to Key West and it looked like a direct hit. The island was in full preparation and evacuation mode. It was already extremely windy. 30-knot winds already and the eye of the storm was still miles away.

Ronnie knew he had to figure this out before the storm hit. Once that happened, there would be no power and truly no way to help Kelly. The phone lines would be down, the cell tower wouldn't work. No electricity at all.

Ronnie plugged his cell in. When the power went out, he had to be ready and fully charged.

He started to scroll through all of his contacts. Looking for someone, anyone that could help his girl.

The wind was really picking up. The storm didn't have to be on top of the island for everyone to lose power. A 50-knot wind and its lights out. They weren't far off.

Ronnie was watching the Miami news station and continuing to scroll through his contacts at the same time. He realized at this point, he needed someone that was south of Cuba to help. Coming anywhere from mainland USA and going into Cuba would be impossible. Maybe for weeks. If Kelly had made it through the storm, there's a pretty good chance she might be injured and with no power or heavy damage to Cuba, she could die while waiting for medical attention.

Of course, Ronnie never thought in a million years that she was in jail. Never.

He kept scrolling. He had several thousand contacts.

All of a sudden it clicked and he stopped scrolling. He stopped breathing.

Couldn't believe that he hadn't thought of this yet.

His publisher friend Larry was in Jamaica. Ocho Rio, Jamaica. He spent a lot of time there. Lived there, if Ronnie remembered correctly more than half the year.

Jamaica had lucked out and was completely missed by Horacio. Some wind. Branches down. But that was it. They never even lost power.

Ronnie started frantically looking for Larry's number. He was sure he had it. He got to the L's and looked for Larry. Larry. Larry. C'mon, Larry. Nothing.

Ronnie was getting pissed. He believed he was running out of time.

"Where the fuck are you, Larry?!" He yelled at the phone. He looked through that whole phone. Searched by first and last name. Both were L's. His name was Larry Lawrence.

Ronnie sat down hard in his recliner. Beginning to

feel defeated. And then ....

It hit him. He had nicknames for just about everyone. He hated Larry. Couldn't stand him in fact. Larry was one of those annoying people who you couldn't shut up. Always running his mouth. You never got a word in edge wise.

He didn't call him Larry. Not behind his back. Behind his back he called him, "Jamaican Jerk"

Ronnie sat up and scrolled to the J's. It didn't take long.

There it was "Jamaican Jerk"

876-235-1032

Bam! Got it.

Maybe, just maybe the Jamaican jerk could help. Larry loved Ronnie. He just didn't know Ronnie couldn't stand him.

The jerk was always trying to impress Ronnie. Always asking him to come stay with him for a week or two. The jerk might actually come in handy, Ronnie thought. Finally it paid off to know a jerk.

CHAPTER 23

Scared In Cuba.

SHE DIDN'T THINK THERE was any way out. This was bad. What are they doing? What are they *going* to do?

Kelly was really scared. How the hell did this happen? All she's trying to do is find her Dad. She never thought in a million years that she would end up in a Cuban jail.

She thought about all she had been through and seen and discovered in the last day or so. She witnessed 2 crew members washed over board during a hurricane and the captain of the ship, who she'd figure out soon enough, was her freaking uncle. Then to make it through all of that and now be locked up in a filthy cell in what she was guessing was Havana.

Perfect

She closed her eyes and thought of home. Of work. Of how simple and easy life was back on her little island home.

Of Ronnie.

She knew, always knew, that she was in love with him. She never wanted to admit it, but she was. She missed him now so much. He'd know what to do. He'd get her out of this mess. She wished he had come with her. But then again, who's to say he wouldn't have been washed aboard himself. She shuddered at the thought.

Any pain to Ronnie caused her pain.

That was love.

She rested her head against the wall and kept her eyes closed. She thought of Ronnie and her out at Fort Zach having a picnic as the gentle ocean breeze washed over them and the sound of tiny waves licking the beach quickly.

Why did she do this? It was so like Kelly to make a rash decision. What did it matter? She barely remembered the

93

man who was her father. She gave up on him a long time ago. Said goodbye a long time ago. She remembers that service at St. Mary's Star of The Sea like it was yesterday.

It was over. All she wrote. She moved on with her life with no father. As time went on the pain lessened. Life has a way of moving shit forward without you even noticing.

So she chased after a man she hardly knew to a place she'd never been, crossed an ocean, almost got killed in a hurricane or even eaten by a shark like poor Uncle Joe. And for this.

Her father obviously didn't give a shit about her, why'd she care so much about him.

Daddy's little girl. There's truth to that. She was daddy's little girl. She followed him everywhere and was madly in love with her Pop.

That's why.

Chasing unrequited love.

Trying to fill that void left by a father who only was thinking of himself. A greedy father. A felon. A crook. An asshole.

Why risk her life for him?

She knew the answer. Because maybe there was a reason for all of it. She didn't know his side of the story after all. Maybe he still loved her as much as she loved him.

She had to know.

The yearning brought her across an ocean in a hurricane.

She was startled out of her daydream by keys rattling and heavy footsteps. She bolted upright and waited for the human that those keys belonged to and the human with those heavy footsteps.

CHAPTER 24

Jamaican Jerk.

THE PHONE CALL TO THE JERK was ringing. One ring. Jerks don't answer the phone after one ring. They want people to think they're busy when everyone knows damn well they're sitting there watching the name flash on screen.

Two rings.

"C'mon, asshole. Answer the damn phone!", Ronnie was after all a very impatient man.

Three

A click.

He knew what was coming next. Voicemail.

He was thrilled to hear what this greeting was going to sound like.

As soon as he heard the jerks voice, it all came back to him. He remembered very clearly now why he couldn't stand this guy. Such an obnoxious tool.

"HEY! Guess what? I missed your call! Oh too bad for you. I'm probably on the beach in JAMAICA BABY! Leave a message and if I got the time, you'll get the call back! Ciao!"

That was the jerk in all his royal jerkiness.

Now Ronnie thought quickly of a non sarcastic hateful message that he wanted to leave and present a more friendly Ronnie who is sympathetic to jerks.

Although, Ronnie really *did* need this guys help. The wellbeing of Kelly relied on the next few seconds of this voicemail.

Ronnie cleared his mind and his throat.

"Hey Larry. How are you, man? Been a long time. This is Ronnie. Man, I really need your help. I think my girl is stuck in Cuba and I don't know what the hell is going on there. Buddy, please give me a call back as soon as you can. Time is not on my side here. I need you buddy. Call me back."

That little 15 second voice message gave Ronnie a headache. That made him feel like he desperately needed a hot shower.

But then he thought of Kelly. Maybe all alone.

That waste of air Jack couldn't have taken very good care of her. He hadn't had a haircut or a shave in 3 years. Couldn't take care of himself for God sake.

Ronnie had to stay busy. He made sure the phone was still plugged in and charging.

He turned the volume up on the TV news for the first time. It was wall to wall hurricane coverage.

Christ, this was a huge storm.

Coming right at us, he thought. Would be on top of us by late afternoon, he thought.

Ronnie never really had a hurricane plan. Never went to the store and stocked up on can goods or water. He never felt a need. Plenty of storms come Key West's way and plenty of them go right on by. But *this* storm was different. It was damn big.

Ronnie decided to take the car to the store. He didn't use the car much. Hardly at all really. Except when he had to be somewhere and it was raining. Nothing worse than getting a wet ass on a scooter.

He headed down the boulevard to the nearest Publix. There was two of em now. A half a block apart. Ronnie never quite understood that. But he liked the newer Publix. Just a tad nicer. He found a parking spot pretty close to the door and walked in. Grabbed a cart and headed to the can food section. The place was *packed*!

Everyone was doing the same thing. Stocking up.

The only thing Ronnie hated more than the

grocery store were all the people inside the grocery store.

He went as fast as he could. Basically just pushing cans into the cart and moving on. Water was a must too. He had been inside the store all of 5 minutes and his cart was almost full. That's the kind of thing that happens when all you care about is getting back outside to freedom.

He checked out and took the offer from one of the bag kids to help him with all his shit out to the car.

After giving the kid a five dollar bill, Ronnie was on his way.

He hadn't even gotten out of the parking lot and his cell rang. It startled him. He was in a zone.

He looked down and there, in big letters, the phone screamed back to him, "Jamaican Jerk"

CHAPTER 25

The Size Of A Small 7-11.

THE STEPS GOT CLOSER. It wasn't a long hallway. Wasn't a big building. It was about the size of a small 7-11. Kelly's cell was at the far end opposite the office area where the cops were. As soon as the cop showed his face, Kelly knew she was in some kind of trouble. His face was a face of anger and evil.

Soon he stood in front of the cell. Staring at her. His glare gave her goosebumps. Sent a shiver down her spine.

All that she had been through, this was the most frightened she'd been.

The jailer stood glaring at Kelly. Then the smile. A cockeyed smirk that terrified Kelly. She stared back, afraid to take her eyes off him but even more afraid to look away.

"Ahhhh, mujer caliente." He spoke.

Kelly didn't speak Spanish, but knew Caliente was hot and mujer was woman. She did *not* want to be a hot woman as this point in her life. Not here, not now.

She wasn't too crazy about being called a hot woman anywhere really.

The jailer sneered into the cell.

Within just a few seconds, he had the key to the cell in his hand and was fumbling to fit it into the locked door.

"Don't even think about it!! Leave me alone."

He laughed. Louder now. He must be all alone. No other cop would allow this too happen. Whatever this was.

He walked into the cell and up to Kelly. They were now just about eye to eye. Her chin was quivering. She had never been close to this scared before in her life.

He reached out his hand quickly enough to make Kelly flinch. He put his hand on her breast. As she tried to squirm away, she realized she was now pinned up against the wall. She had no choice but to just stand and hope for best.

His smile became more diabolical. He squeezed her breast as he breathed heavily. She could smell cheap rum and cigar on his breath. Not a good smell.

Kelly thought this is it. I'm going to be raped in a Cuban jail.

But the jailer had other ideas. Without talking his hand off her breast, with the other hand he smacked her hard across the face. So hard it made Kelly's knees buckle.

Oh God Oh God Oh God, was all that was going through her mind.

Before the sting went away from the slap, here came another. And another. And another. As he slapped her, his grin and laugh grew louder. His breathing quicker.

It seemed like a second or two and he was not only slapping her he was punching now too. Not just her face but all over her body. One punch knocked the wind out of her. She could hardly find the breath to scream, but she did her best. She squealed out the best scream she could. But the beating continued.

Why is this happening? she thought. Why!?

She couldn't breathe. She hurt all over her body. She could feel warmth coming from her lip and forehead. Then she tasted the unmistakable flow of blood.

She was in real danger of dying right there in that cell.

Then she heard a door slamming. Was that the front door or the cell door or something else. The beating didn't stop. The jailer was hitting her so much, it felt as if three jailers were beating her. She felt surrounded.

"Javier!! Enough!!!"

All at once it was over. The beating stopped abruptly.

The jailer spun around to see the Chief. The first guy that grabbed Kelly on the beach. He swung the door to the cell open and stood as "Javier" walked slowly out, but not before one final hard squeeze to her breast. This guy was sadistic.

As he walked out of the cell, the chief gave him a hard slap to the back of the head. Hard enough that Javier stumbled a few steps out of the cell.

Kelly lay a crumpled heap on the floor.

"Lo siento. Una enfermera estará pronto."

Kelly knew sorry and nurse.

She knew it was over.

She had never been beaten like this and hurt from head to toe.

She looked up at the Chief and said, "gracias"

CHAPTER 26

SOB.

"**H**ELLO?"

"Ronnie!! You sonofabitch! How the hell are you?!"

Ronnie had to hold the phone away from his ear. Another sign of an asshole. Not knowing how loud he is on the damn phone!

"Hey Larry. Thanks for getting back to me."

"No worries, man. Your voicemail sounded like you were in a jam, what can I do for you?"

"Well, long story short ... I think my girl went to Cuba and got caught in that storm. I'm not sure if she made it or not. She may be in Cuba and I'm really worried about her."

Larry took a deep breath, "Holy shit, man! I can't imagine anyone surviving that storm out there."

Perfect. Exactly what Ronnie wanted to hear. God he hated this man. But if his plan worked and he got to Kelly, he'd put up with him as long as it took.

"Yea, I hear ya. But I gotta believe she made it. I can't get there with this storm coming right at us, but I thought maybe you could."

"Oh man, Ronnie, that's gonna be tough. I mean where would I even start to look for her?"

"Well, the first natural place she'd most likely hit is Havana."

"So, what exactly are you asking me here?"

What a fucking idiot. What did he think Ronnie wanted? To go to Havana and buy him some cigars?

Ronnie clenched his fish, "Man, I need you to go to Cuba and try and find her. I'll pay whatever you need to get it done. I'll wire you as much cash as you need."

Larry took an audible breath. Cash had a way of convincing people. An unlimited supply of cash normally got you whatever you needed. God knows Ronnie had plenty of cash.

"Well, to make that trip and all the expense ... I mean I'd have to get a hotel room, charter a little plane, that would probably cost me around 5 grand."

5 grand? Really?! You fucking son of a bitch, Ronnie thought. He was clenching his teeth now.

"Alright. I can do that. Where do you want me to wire it. I can western union it."

"Yea that would be perfect. Send it right to the hotel here. In the meantime I'll get packed and book a flight, could be in Cuba in a few hours ... depending on how long it'll take you to get me the cash.

"I'll have it to you within the hour."

Ronnie realized he couldn't use western union for that kind of money. It would have to be bank to bank. He dreaded the idea of calling this prick back. But he did.

And after several painful more minutes, he had the jerk's bank info.

Ronnie hopped on the scooter without thinking and took off for the bank.

CHAPTER 27

Selena.

KELLY SAT ON THE FLOOR inside that Cuban jail. She was hurting all over. She was bleeding. She was confused about how all this was happening. She didn't think Americans were an enemy to Cuba. Why was she being roughed up, taken to jail, and assaulted?

She started to cry. Not something that she did a lot. She was the kind of woman who kept things bottled up inside. She couldn't help it though.

As the tears starting to sting as they rolled down her face she started to think about her father. How he'd feel knowing that his only daughter had been through all of this just to find him.

Kelly didn't sob. She just quietly cried. She regretted all of it. She regretted hearing the news from that asshole Jack/Joe. She regretted having a fight with Ronnie. She regretted ever spending a thousand dollars to get on that ill fated boat.

Now here she was. Beaten, bloodied, assaulted, dirty, tired, hungry and all alone. She didn't know what was going to happen and where all this would end up.

Kelly wasn't a religious person, but at this point, she quietly talked to God, "Dear God, if you can hear me, please help me out of this. All I wanted to do was find my Daddy. I don't deserve this God. I'm a good person. Please, Dear Lord, help me," she cried even harder now. "Please God, help me."

At that point, maybe purely by coincidence, there were footsteps coming down the hall. Heavy footsteps.

Oh God please don't let this be that maniac, she thought.

A figure arrived at the door. It was El Jefe. The Chief. Someone was with him. A much smaller silhouette. It was a woman. She was wearing white.

The nurse.

"Hi, dear. I'm the nurse and we're going to get you cleaned up a little." She spoke English, with a heavy Cuban accent, but English nonetheless.

The Chief spoke to the nurse, briefly, gruffly, and then walked away. The nurse walked into the cell. "My name is Selena. How are you feeling, dear?"

"Awful, just awful."

"I'm so sorry this has happened to you. But I'm going to do the best I can to make you feel a little better, ok?"

"Ok." Kelly was surprised to hear the desperation in her own voice.

Selena was Kelly's best friend in the whole world right now. She was her only chance to maybe get out of here.

"Ok, dear, let's get you standing and over to the sink."

Kelly, with assistance, stood up and immediately almost fell over. Her legs were like spaghetti. She couldn't feel anything beneath her waist. She felt as though she was still on the wobbly old boat.

"C'mon, dear. Take your time. You can do this. He really did a number on you didn't he?"

The kindness that Selena was showing Kelly right now made her cry. It was so nice to finally have an ally. It was nice to finally have someone that was going to treat her like a human being.

"The chief just fired Javier. This kind of thing has happened before. He gave him the option of leaving or being arrested. He left. He's a very sick man that doesn't belong on the street. I'm sorry this happened to you", She muttered again. Kelly felt like Selena really *was* sorry this happened.

If Javier did this kind of thing before, this must not be the first time she had to bandage someone up.

The water that came out of the faucet came very slowly. Just a trickle really. The water had a brown tinge to it. Kelly didn't care. She had no plans to drink it, she just wanted to feel better.

Very slowly, Selena started cleaning the dried blood off Kelly's face, hands, head and legs. She really was a mess. She didn't think she had any broken bones, but boy it felt like it.

After around 30 or 40 minutes, Selena finished up and Kelly was now going to make her way back to the all metal bed, a bench really, with no mattress or pillow or blanket.

"I'm going to see if I can get you a pillow and blanket, ok, dear?"

"Yes, thank you so much." Kelly was so thankful for Selena that she started to cry again. She so appreciated her kindness and soft touch over all the cuts, abrasions and bruises.

Selena leaned in, "After I get bedding, we'll see about getting you out of here. Ok, Dear?"

Kelly just nodded. She didn't know how a nurse was going to get her out of jail, but she didn't question it.

She actually became a little hopeful that maybe this wasn't going to last much longer.

CHAPTER 28

Larry on the Way.

THE MONEY TRANSFER WAS COMPLETE. 5 grand on its way to Hermosa Cove resort in Jamaica. 5 grand on its way to the chubby little hands of the jerk. The one man standing between Ronnie and finding Kelly safe.

He couldn't believe that he was putting all his hope in this fool's hands. But what choice did he have. This guy was it. He didn't know anyone else or any other way. He thought, Believe me if knew another way I'd be doing it.

Ronnie thought back when he first met the jerk. It was at a publisher's office in a swanky 5th avenue office. He hated him almost instantly. As soon as he walked in with his flowery shirt and khakis. Looking like he just rolled off a hammock in Jamaica. Who knew?

Larry, the jerk, seemed like he worked hard enough, problem was he played even harder. He was one of those guys with his shirt opened way too far. Way too much chest hair and a gaudy thick gold chain. A gold bracelet and a gold pinky ring. All things that Ronnie hated. And to make matters worse, Larry was way too heavy to pull any of this look together.

He had been married *five* times! His ex wives were all beautiful. What did they see in this freak-show? It was hard to imagine.

So just seeing Larry, Ronnie hated him. He hadn't even opened his big mouth yet. But of course, that was coming. As the jerk entered the same sprawling office, his first words were, "Ronnie, baby. What a damn pleasure it is to meet you!!"

Good grief. Ronnie look at his publisher and rolled his eyes. His eyes said, "*This* is the guy you want me to work with?! Really!

The rest of that conversation Ronnie has no recollection of. He blocked it out like a dog blocks out the last time you smacked it on the ass. He does remember when the jerk left. That conversation that took place with the publisher.

"John, are you fucking kidding me?! If you push that asshole on me, I will never write another book for this company again. Ever!"

And now this asshole was going to be on his way to Cuba to help find his love, Kelly.

CHAPTER 29

Some Relief.

TRUE TO HER WORD Selena came back. This time she was with the chief and another nurse dressed in white. The chief, who Kelly thought looked the meanest, had a much softer face than she had first realized. They all had a look of pity on their face.

Now no Conch ever wants pity from anyone, but Kelly was in a bit of a pickle and had no problem with pity if it meant getting out of this stank cell and getting help.

Selena, the only one who spoke English clearly, spoke first.

"Ok, dear. We're going to take you to the hospital. Gonna get you fixed up and feeling better, ok?"

"Yes ma'am." Kelly would always have those conch manners.

They brought a wheel chair into the cell and very gently lifted Kelly in. They backed out of the small cell and wheeled her down the short dark hallway to the bright sunlight peering through the open front door.

Kelly had to shield her eyes from the bright Cuban sun. But she could clearly see an ambulance parked in front with the loud engine running waiting to transport her to safety.

As the ambulance rumbled towards the hospital, Kelly began to think. She thought about what she was even doing here. What she had hoped to find. She wished she had listened to Ronnie. Wished she hadn't acted so rash. Wished that asshole, Jack or Joe or whoever the fuck he was would've talked her out of the trip. But most of all, she truly missed Ronnie.

They had been through a lot. She knew she was in love with Ronnie a long time ago but was pretty certain he only looked at her as the cleaning girl. With benefits.

She wished she were back in Ronnie's little apartment that she loved so much taking a day nap with Ronnie lying next to her as the cool breeze from the window AC slipped over them. The music from Ronnie's Pandora playing some soft jazz. The dogs snoring peacefully at the foot of the bed. She closed her eyes and dreamed about how lovely that was. Funny how we take things for granted, she thought. No matter what happens, things would be different, she thought. She would never take the little things for granted again.

It was a pretty quick, albeit bumpy ride, to the hospital. Kelly couldn't help wondering how lousy this hospital probably was. She was wrong. As they pulled into the driveway, Kelly was shocked to see how decent the hospital looked. She knew that healthcare was free here, and how amazing that hadn't caught on yet in America.

They wheeled her into the Emergency Room. It was white and clean. And relatively quiet. As soon as they got there, a nurse dressed just like Selena, rushed over and in Spanish spoke to Selena and then grabbed the wheelchair and wheeled her into a private exam room. She was left there without so much as a word. It felt like she was there for hours by herself, not knowing what was going on just on the other side of the curtain.

CHAPTER 30

The Jerk Travels.

SO OPERATION JERK WAS IN FULL SWING. The money was in his hands and now would be chartering a plane to Havana. The Jerk had a very real complaint. How the hell was he going to find Kelly and where would he even start. Havana isn't a small place, especially when you're looking for a needle like Kelly.

The Jerk had already reached out to the pilot, a buddy of his supposedly. The pilots name was Bill. So Bill the pilot and Larry the Jerk would shortly be on their way to find Kelly.

Ronnie felt so helpless. He wished he could be on that plane. That he would be the one to touch down in Havana. That he could be the one who spotted Kelly and then brought her home to Key West.

But alas, it was the Jerk and some guy named Bill. Bill was from England. He's been flying planes since he was a boy. Everyone in his inner circle called him English Bill. Original.

It was a sunny warm day when English Bill and the Jerk decided to take off. Not a cloud in the sky. It would be a quick hop to Havana airport and then the real hard work would begin. Literally trying to find a needle in a haystack. But when thought about, a white girl in a country of much darker people ... maybe it wouldn't be so hard.

English Bill and the Jerk loaded up that little Cessna and prepared for take off. As they started down the runway, they had no idea what Ronnie already was paying attention to back home in Key West.

Horacio had taken a wobble. A wobble east. Heading right in the direction of ... Jamaica.

CHAPTER 31

The Doctor Will See You Now.

KELLY HAD BEEN IN THAT LITTLE ROOM in this little hospital in Cuba for what seemed like at least an hour. She was about to push herself out into the hallway and holler for help. She couldn't bear it any longer. Just when she was ready to make a break for it, the doctor walked in and said hello.

Kelly was taken aback a little when he walked in. For one, he was very young. And two, he was incredibly handsome. Maybe the most handsome man she'd ever seen. He was tall, maybe 6 feet or so. Thin, but muscular. A beautiful full head of jet black hair. High cheekbones and most importantly, his eyes. They were the darkest most soulful eyes she'd ever seen. Surrounded by long eyelashes.

This man could be on the cover of GQ. Kelly struggled to pull herself together. As beat up and sore as she was, she was very happy that this man was the man that would offer relief from her pain. Her physical pain that is.

"I see you've had a bad day, yes?" Asked the model doctor. When Kelly spoke, in her head her voice was much louder. But came out like a squeak from a mouse.

"Yes, excuse me (louder) Yes. You could say that."

"What happened to you my dear?"

Here's where Kelly didn't know what to do. Did she tell the truth and tell the handsome doctor that she was beat in a jail by a bad cop or make up some, I fell down the stairs crap.

"Well, I was beaten in the jail," she said meekly with her head down.

"I see", said handsome doctor, "I have heard of that kind of thing happening in that jail before."

"Well they fired the cop that did this to me."

"That is very good to hear." His English was near perfect but he still had quite a Cuban accent. But those eyes. She knew she was staring, but guessed he got that a lot.

"Let's take a look at those injuries."

Kelly became nervous, but handsome doctor was so gentle and so incredibly professional she was at ease within minutes. The nurse, Selena, walked in and assisted him. She helped Kelly to move around the room and the examining table. Selena was also a very sweet person who took her job very seriously.

The exam took around an hour or so. Selena would pay attention to one area and the handsome doctor would point out something else and she would get busy cleaning wounds and taking care not to hurt Kelly too much.

At the end of the exam, Selena said it was the best they could do. And that Kelly needed plenty of rest. She suggested she should be admitted to the hospital where she could receive plenty of attention and plenty of rest.

After what Kelly had been through that actually didn't sound bad. She was exhausted. And for one fleeting moment she almost said ok, but then she remembered why she was here. What her mission was. She had to find Dad. Had to get the answers that were rolling around in her head for the last 48 hours.

"As nice as it sounds to get some rest, I have a mission that I came to Cuba for. I came in search of my father. I haven't seen him in a very long time. He's from Key West like me and I heard he was here."

"Your father's name wouldn't be Frank would it?"

Kelly would now need some stitches from handsome doctor because she fell over in the wheelchair and hit her head on the floor. She lost consciousness. Her last thought was, "Holy shit!!"

CHAPTER 32

The Return of Horacio.

RONNIE WAS WATCHING the weather channel in stunned silence. He was shaking. He was mad and sad and terrified all at the same time. This could not be happening, he thought. HOW could this be happening, he thought.

This monster hurricane named Horacio had taken a mean wobble east and was headed right towards Jamaica. He was stunned. There's no way English Bill and the Jerk could possibly know this. It was a tiny Cessna with none of the high tech radar and technology that bigger planes have.

For the first time ever, Ronnie felt bad for calling Larry a jerk. He felt bad that he had sent them on this death mission to Cuba. There could not be a worse case scenario, Ronnie thought.

As he watched the weather channel everything that had happened over the last 2 days started to hit him hard. Forget that his girl was probably dead. Washed over board or worse. Now, he has sent two men to a watery grave trying to find that same girl. Ronnie hadn't cried in years, but now found that he couldn't control it any more.

He broke down. Hard. He hit the floor and there on his knees he sobbed and sobbed. He felt so helpless and hopeless.

CHAPTER 33

Walking Out.

WHEN KELLY WOKE UP she was surrounded by 5 other nurses and one other doctor nowhere near as handsome as handsome doctor. She was now more sore than ever. And now she had 4 stitches above her right eye to boot. She was a mess.

"What did you say about Frank?" Kelly asked Selena.

"The only American from Key West that I know is a man named Frank who has an export business here. He's been here for many years."

"That's got to be my dad!!" Kelly shouted. So loudly that one of the nurses flinched a little.

Kelly quickly had a thought about traveling across an ocean, getting beat up by a cop in a Cuban jail and then the nurse fixing her up knew her dad. Could it really be this easy? Could this nurse know her dad?

"But Frank passed away a few months ago, there was a large funeral procession and half of Havana came out for it."

All at once Kelly's heart sank. A heavy load sat on her chest and she found it hard to breathe. She started crying in a way that most people have never cried. She was heaving large sobs to the point she couldn't see and no one could understand her. And then it all went black again. Kelly didn't know it, but when she woke back up, Selena the nurse would become her best friend in the world.

CHAPTER 34

The Plane, The Plane.

SO WHAT RONNIE THOUGHT would be an ill-fated plane ride was taxiing down the runway, the two passengers were laughing and kidding around. Oblivious to what was out there. Swirling. And huge. Horacio was out there and he was a big blowhard.

English Bill and the Jerk took to the sky on their way to Cuba. It really was a beautiful day. Often that's the case before a big storm. There really was something to the old adage "The calm before the storm".

Before long they were about 4,000 feet up and cruising. Those old little Cessna's were loud as shit. The headphones were a must. The only way the two could hear each other.

They were both in good moods. English Bill had been to Cuba many times but the Jerk had never been. He was excited. Felt like he could bring some cigars and coffee and sugar cane back with him and make some money. Always the money with the Jerk.

The trip from Jamaica to Cuba was about 530 miles. A quick jog but still around 2 hours by plane. The water below was crystal clear and a pretty shade of dark blue, green and turquoise. English Bill loved this view. He felt it was God's work at its finest. If you looked close enough you'd see big fish and sharks and the occasional big sea turtle.

Even though it was starting to cloud up a little bit about an hour in, English Bill wasn't worried at all. Clouds happened all the time and most times it wouldn't even rain. It would be just cloudy.

About 45 minutes out of Cuba it started to rain. A few drops at first, but harder a few minutes later. English Bill had the wipers on as fast as they would go and it was still hard to see. They hit a little turbulence. Same thing. Not so bad at first, but harder a few minutes later.

It was clear to the Jerk that English Bill was struggling. He was a tough guy who'd flown through worse shit, but it was hard keeping things straight.

Of course the Jerk was, you guessed it, a pussy. He started to freak out a little and said to English Bill, "Are we gonna be ok here? This is starting to look pretty rough!"

"Nothing to worry about my boy. We're only about 30 minutes out. We'll be just fine!"

As English Bill said this the Cessna really started to buck. His arms were really struggling to keep a grip now and the Jerk started to sweat. A little at first, harder a few minutes later. He was downright scared. On a bigger plane this would be nothing. A little bumpy but no big deal. On a tiny two seat Cessna it was downright frightening.

The Jerk looked over at English Bill and for the first time he looked worried. He was getting wore out. It was tough hanging on. Neither man said anything to each other. The only sounds were the engine and all the rattling and buzzers.

They were both hanging on for dear life. The Jerk even more so. He had both hands under the seat beneath him just holding on.

"Ok, I'll admit it, this is way worse than I thought, said English Bill, "I don't know how much longer I can hold on!!"

Oh shit! That certainly was the last possible thing the Jerk wanted to hear. He was beyond scared now. Way beyond. He was sweating profusely now and felt like throwing up. He thought about crashing into the ocean and being eaten by sharks. Could there be a worse way to go?

At this point, English Bill realized this was much more than just a thundershower. He knew now, from his years in the air, that they were in the middle of a big damn hurricane. It was then that English Bill knew he didn't have enough in him, as much as he wanted, to fight this storm. He was worn out so bad his arms felt like rubber. It was all he could do just to hang on. His fingers were slipping. He knew it wouldn't be long before he lost control.

"Listen to me, Larry! I think we have to start thinking about a water landing!! I can't hang on much longer and we sure as shit can't fight this hurricane much longer!!"

"This is a hurricane??!!"

The Jerk was a little slow.

"No doubt about it and a big one at that!!"

Just minutes out of Cuba and the engines on that little Cessna gave out.

"We lost the engines!! This is it!!"

The Jerk thought, what the hell do you mean this is it. He really was a tad slow.

"We're gonna go down. It's gonna be a hard landing. Brace yourself. Try to put your head as much between your legs as possible!!"

Larry the Jerk could not believe this was happening. Could this be how it would end? Doing a favor for a guy he barely knew who had given him a lousy 5 grand?

As the Jerk thought of this he noticed they were just a few hundred feet from the ocean. This was going to hurt. Bad.

And then, the impact. The Jerk had never heard such a loud noise. And within just a few seconds the warm ocean water was on top of both of them. This was definitely the end. They both thought the same damn thing.

The Jerk looked over and quickly realized that English Bill was dead. On impact. But Larry was still alive. He had made it through the crash. What now he thought.

The Cessna had leveled out and was now just floating. There was about a foot of water in the cockpit. Both wings were gone. It was just part of the fuselage that remained. The Jerk realized he could possibly make it. Make it out of this mess. Somehow.

It was eerily quiet now. Just the sound of the water. He looked over at Bill again. Yep, he was dead alright.

And now, 20 minutes away from Cuba, in the middle of the ocean, Larry was all alone. Just a jerk in the ocean.

He was more afraid than he'd ever been in his life.

CHAPTER 35

Awake. Now What?

KELLY'S EYES SLOWLY OPENED. She didn't recognize anything really. She didn't quite remember where the hell she was. Then the pain came in waves over her. Now she remembered. It seemed as if every bone in her body was broken and something around her eye was throbbing.

She looked around this very tiny room. It was coming back to her. She started to remember getting beat up. The handsome doctor and Selena. Then as her eyes opened more, she saw Selena standing there. With a smile on her face.

"Good morning, Dear. You scared us a little. It's good to see you open your eyes. Do you know where you are?"

"Cuba. Hospital. Handsome." They were the only words she could muster.

Selena chuckled. "You're really in bad shape. You need to stay put for a week or so and rest. Your injuries are severe."

Then Kelly remembered why she was in Cuba. Daddy. She started sobbing.

"What's the matter, dear. You're safe and in good hands."

"All I wanted to do was find my Daddy and now I'll never see him!"

"Oh dear, I'm so sorry. When you said a man from key west named Frank I thought of a man who came on a boat very often and sank a few months ago. We never found him. I don't think that was your father. I just have a feeling it wasn't."

Kelly's spirits lifted.

"Why don't you think it was my Daddy? My Frank?"

"What is your last name, dear? We've never even asked."

Kelly actually had to stop and think for a moment. She had been through so much, she was having a hard time remembering things.

Then it hit her.

"Alvarez", she said.

"Oh Dear, I'm so sorry I said anything. This mans name was not Alvarez. It was Caprio. Frank Caprio."

CHAPTER 36

Decisions. Decisions.

A S THE PLANE FLOATED ALONG in the Straits, it started to take on more and more water. The Jerk was terrified but came to the conclusion that he would be safer on top of the plane rather than in it.

The trick was getting out of this death grip the safety belt and the crushed fuselage was holding him in.

He looked around for any kind of tool or sharp object that would at least cut him out of the safety belts lock.

As he looked around and up and down, his eyes locked onto a large piece of glass from the front window. He started to reach for it but when he did pain shot up his leg and into his back. He screamed in agony.

"You have got to be kidding me!!" he yelled to no one but the fish. At this point he figured out that shard of glass was his only hope. If he could just stretch across and grab it. He forced himself to stretch further and further. The pain was almost too much. But he grit his teeth and pushed through the pain. With a sound sort of between a scream and a growl, he reached and reached until his hand was on it.

He pulled it in close to him and the shard bit him. Hard. He didn't even realize he was cut and bleeding until he looked down and saw his $250 pleated pants soaked in red. The cut wasn't too bad, looked worse than it was. The Jerk took off his outer shirt and wrapped part of it around the shard of glass and part of it around the wound on his hand.

He started to saw into the safety belt. To no avail. That belt was thick and heavy. But the Jerk knew he had to get out of there. This was his only option. So he kept at it. Kept sawing and sawing. After 30 minutes or so he looked down to see the belt was starting to fray. It was working. He let out a little "Yes!" to celebrate this victory. He paused to catch his breath and wipe the sweat off his head and out of his eyes.

The belt cut easy from that point. He cut hard for another few minutes until, POP! It finally cut loose. He was free. Kind of.

His chore now was getting out of this thing before the water completely covered the door. Thankfully the plane was leaning to the opposite side so he didn't have to push against too much water.

He grabbed onto the door handle and gave it a push. Nothing. No movement at all. The Jerk was in a great deal of agony but knew he had to get out of this plane before he drowned inside of it.

He finally leaned into the door and with his last bit of strength pushed hard and it popped open. The water rushed in. He had to move fast. The Jerk wasn't known for his athletic ability that's for sure, but his life was depending on him getting out of the plane and on top of that plane before he drowned.

He sort of fell into the warm water and before he knew it he almost lost control. The water was deeper than he thought. He assumed he'd be able to touch the ground maybe and easily hop up onto the plane. That was not the case. It took effort. A lot of effort. He had to tread water while finding a place to grip onto and then with the water to his waist he had to pull himself up.

It was like pulling a wet towel out of the pool. Not

easy. Heavy. But again, the thought of him dying out here was something he refused to allow. As it turns out the Jerk had some balls ... at least when it came to saving his own ass.

CHAPTER 37

Oops. Wrong Name.

KELLY WAS SHOCKED. She couldn't believe this roller coaster she was on. Her father's dead and then alive, then he's dead again and now he's alive.

Jesus, God.

She could see the pain on Selena's face. She felt horrible that she had told Kelly "her" father had died. Kelly wasn't mad at her. How could she be? She had been such help and comfort to her.

The question now remained. When can she get out of here and where is her father? It started to settle with her where she would even start. Havana wasn't huge but it sure wasn't small either. It was strange that Kelly was having the same thought about her Dad as Ronnie was having about her.

First thing was first though, Kelly had to be strong enough to leave this hospital on her own free will. She also started to get that she was not strong enough to leave. Not on her own.

"Selena, I have to find my Dad. Can you think of anyway I can do that? Where do I even start?" In the last 48 hours Kelly had cried more than maybe her whole life. She felt it coming again while she asked that question.

Selena knew Kelly was hurting. Emotionally and physically. She knew she could help the bruises and cuts but was at a loss as to how to help find her father.

"Dear I just don't know. That is a hard task. There are many places that someone can hide if they don't want to be found."

Kelly sort of knew that's the answer she would get.

Selena was right. Kelly was starting to feel hopeless. Starting to feel like this was a lost cause.

What was she thinking? Traveling across an ocean with less than a day of planning. Without even checking the weather. Without so much as a clue as to what she would do when she arrived.

Kelly was in trouble. Serious trouble. In a strange land with dangerous people who would have no trouble hurting her. That much has already been proven.

And another thing. How many men known as Alvarez must live on this island? 10? 20? 100?

It was hopeless.

Kelly was lost in the truest sense of the word.

CHAPTER 38

Can a Jerk Swim?

NIGHT WAS BEGINNING TO FALL. It was already shaping up to be one of those once in a lifetime sunsets. He thought about laying out at the hotel pool and watching. Waiting to maybe see the green flash that so many talked about. A very elusive green light right as the sun touched the horizon. He'd only seen pictures.

But lying out at the hotel pool at sunset. Looking at the ocean and watching the sun take its last dip. Boy it was something. As he grew more and more tired he thought about how badly he wanted to be doing that again. He also, for the millionth time cursed fucking Ronnie.

He didn't even know Ronnie that well. He made some money off him but he was barely a flicker on the jerks calendar. And now that fucker was about to kill him. Not directly of course, but because of this hair brained idea of trying to find his god damn girlfriend in a virtually unknown place.

Back to the sunset. He had to calm down. He needed his energy. Every ounce. Because he was quickly seeing this slippery climb to the top of the plane was going to be damn near impossible.

The Jerk swam out just a hair further. To get a better look at the challenge before him. It looked even worse from back aways. How the hell was he going to do this, he thought.

Then, like a bolt of lightning, the Jerk saw them. Steps! Steps that would reach almost to the top. Steps that would make this challenge seem possible. He could've slapped himself in the face for being so stupid not noticing before. He almost started to cry he was so relieved.

He swam closer to the side of the wrecked Cessna and began to climb the steps. Slippery as shit on hot pavement, but he very slowly made the ascent.

CHAPTER 39

Action.

THERE RONNIE WAS ON THE FLOOR of his tiny apartment under a sapodilla tree in Key West, Florida ... balling. After what seemed like a half an hour, Ronnie pulled himself up and started to wipe away the tears that hadn't come since the 90's. He got to thinking.

He had a lot of money. More than he could ever spend. And more was coming every month. Around 100 grand or so every month from all his *New York Times* bestselling books. For the first time Ronnie thanked God for all those idiots that bought his books.

Maybe the Jerk made it and maybe he didn't, Ronnie thought. The guy was, after all, a jerk. Jerks fail. Often. Larry the Jerk had always fallen ass backwards into money with very little personal effort.

So. Maybe he did make it. He had to be the luckiest SOB on the planet. To have as much money as he had with almost no brain power was a miracle. Maybe the ol Jerk still had a little left in him.

But Ronnie felt like he couldn't chance it. There had to be a way he could also make it to Cuba. A boat was out of the effin question. But his own chartered plane??? Maybe.

Ronnie reached out to his favorite meteorologist at the national weather service right there in Key West. Maybe she could tell him where the storm was and if there was any way to get a plane into Cuba. Lilly was her name and she was sharp as a tack. Incredibly smart. She was a weather scientist. She also knew people in town. Maybe people looking to make a few thousand dollars to fly him near a hurricane and into Cuba.

She also adored Kelly. Most people did, but Lilly thought the world of Kelly. She knew all the stories like everyone else and she never looked down on Kelly or thought any less of her. She really loved her. Ronnie doubted Lilly knew what was going on with Kelly.

The phone rang. Once. Twice. Three goddamn times.

"Hello, National Weather Service, this is Lilly how can I help you?"

"Lil, this is Ronnie. I got a real problem."

"Jesus, Ronnie, not even a proper hello?"

"Listen Lil, seriously. Kelly went off to Cuba in a boat with Captain Jack. I think she went right into that storm. I gotta find a way to fly over the ocean and maybe find her or better yet get to Cuba and look for her there."

"Holy shit, Ronnie, this is a huge storm!! No one could've survived it, especially on a boat!" Lilly realized what she had just said and that she said it to a man who loved Kelly.

"I'm sorry honey. It's just hard to imagine anyone making it through the other side of that storm."

"Where is it now? Is it far enough away from Cuba where I can charter a plane there relatively safely?"

"It's a couple hundred miles away, but still creating some real bad weather for Cuba."

"Ya think I could get there, Lilly! Answer me straight for Christ sake!!"

Now it was Ronnie's turn to realize who he was talking to. A lady that could really help him.

"I'm sorry, Lil, I'm just so god damn worried about her. I don't know what else to do!"

"I understand. I'm scared for her too. I mean,

under the right circumstances and with a whole shit ton of luck you might be able to get in there. But it would take a lot of skill from a pilot and a whole lot of luck!"

"Yea, you mentioned the luck part already. But you didn't say I couldn't or shouldn't do it."

"Oh you definitely should NOT do it. It's incredibly dangerous. I wouldn't let my worst enemy go near there. This is still a very strong storm and it's a storm with a real fucking attitude."

"Lilly I gotta try. I have to do something. I can't bear the thought that she's hanging on to some piece of boat floating in the ocean somewhere. I gotta try. I just have to."

CHAPTER 40

On Her Way.

KELLY HAD SLEPT FOR HOURS. She woke feeling sore but much better. Selena told her all she did was toss and turn. But Kelly knew she slept hard. She dreamed about Frank. Frankie. Dad. She dreamed about finding him. About bringing him home and if not home just having him be a part of her life again. That's the one thing she wanted more than anything.

Of course all this would happen after the kick to the balls. He deserved it. Who knows maybe he has a good excuse, even though Kelly couldn't think of one. Not even close to one. What could possibly make a man up and leave his family. Fake his own death. She really couldn't think of anything that would make a man do that. Especially an Alvarez man.

As it turned out while Kelly was asleep, Selena had been doing some pretty hardcore re-com type stuff. She had reached out to everyone she could think of to see if they knew of or had ever heard of a Frank Alvarez from Key West. Most said no. One said maybe.

A man like Frank Alvarez couldn't possibly hide in Cuba no matter how hard he tried. If he were here, he would have to reach out to someone local. No one can ever be completely off the grid for ever. Maybe those Japanese guys hiding in the jungle still thinking the war was going on. But otherwise, it would be hard.

Somebody would have to know. If he was in Cuba at all.

Kelly started to think of the possibility that she was in the wrong place. That maybe he wasn't in Cuba after all. That thought almost made her puke.

But Selena, who at this point was Kelly's best friend, her only friend, has been busy. Had made lots of calls and talked to a lot of locals. She had actually left the hospital and rode around the island on her bicycle to see if she could find anything out about this strange man.

All the way on the other side of Havana, the more remote part of town, she got the maybe. She took a cab to get there. One of those old '57 Chevys. It was pink. Too far to bike.

Plus she had heard from one source that there was an older white man living there. An old white man who kept to himself, but seemed to be in business of some kind. He seemed to have a lot of money.

This was the lead that Selena was following. She was doing it for Kelly. That sweet American girl sleeping for the first time in 2 days back at the hospital. Selena felt so bad for bringing up the wrong Frank. She felt she had to do more for Kelly. She felt like she knew enough people, almost everyone in Havana, that she could find something. Anything. Maybe Frank Alvarez himself.

As the pink '57 Chevy pulled into a very jungle looking area, the cab driver said this was as far as he could go. Selena would have to hoof it from here. She had no idea where she was going. But she felt something. Felt like she was in the right place. Selena was a devout Christian and believed that everything happened for a reason. That God put paths in people's lives for a reason. To follow them.

Selena went with her heart leading the way. As she walked down the dirt path, she saw smoke. A lot of smoke. She knew at that point that someone was living down this dirt path. And god only knew what it led to, maybe Kelly's long lost father.

Selena trudged on. Towards that smoke.

CHAPTER 41

On Top of the World.

THE JERK, AFTER A LONG TIME and much effort, had finally made it on top of the plane. He could see for miles up there. And he actually felt much safer too.

He knew there had to be sharks in that warm water. He didn't want to stick around to find out. The sun was even closer to the horizon now. He figured there might be 2 or 3 more hours of light. He had hoped that someone from above would spot the wreckage and him on top of it.

He knew he was all alone on top of this plane. Time was not on his side. He thought there was no way he could spend the night out here. And he was hungry and super thirsty on top of it.

He was all alone with his thoughts too. First thing he thought of was that asshole Ronnie who got him into this mess to begin with. Second thing. Sunset at his hotel. He closed his eyes and thought about lying out by the pool and watching the pretty girls in their skimpy bikinis walking by and watching that sun set.

Before long it was dusk. The sun was almost gone and The Jerk got worried, really worried, that he was going to indeed spend the night out here.

He wondered how long he could go without water. He knew he could go a long time without food, but what about water.

What a fucked up thing. Being surrounded by water that you can't drink. A big fucking cosmic joke. A joke that the Jerk didn't find funny at all.

Then. Darkness. It felt like it happened so quickly.

Here the Jerk was, Larry, on top of a plane wreck in the middle of the ocean about to spend the night here. The Jerk would've never admitted to anyone that he was indeed terrified of the dark.

And the dark that was coming was darker, blacker than any dark he had ever seen. Out in the middle of the ocean, all you see are stars. All you hear is the ocean. If he was on some sort of wilderness excursion he might find this very peaceful. But he wasn't. He was alone with the ocean and the ocean could be a real asshole.

CHAPTER 42

Action. Finally.

RONNIE HAD FOUND A GUY in Key West, thanks to Lilly, with some balls. He had a small seaplane and wasn't afraid to fly near the storm. It was going to cost Ronnie though. $10,000. Ronnie had it, but was a little pissed that this guy was making him spend it. But really Ronnie could care less. All he was thinking about was his girl. He had to get to her before it was too late.

The pilots name Freddie. Freddie was a long time local with deep roots in Key West. And Freddie was a bona fide bad-ass. He had balls the size of grapefruits and flew some pretty crazy missions during the Vietnam War. He was up to the challenge, especially with his pocket bulging with Ronnie's ten g's.

Ronnie drove out to the tiny airfield where Freddie flew out of. It was about 10 miles up the Keys. He had called beforehand and talked to Freddie so Freddie was expecting him.

The sun was going down though and Ronnie thought if he was going to go he'd have to go now.

He pulled into the gravel driveway with a car he borrowed from his dear friend Peter who was always available to lend a hand.

About half way down the driveway, he saw a man. This had to be Freddie. He was a short man with a head full of nothing but white hair. He had a mischievous look about him. An easy smile and rather good looking. For his age anyway.

Ronnie got out of the car and introduced himself. They shook hands and Ronnie liked Freddie immediately. He could tell just by the handshake that Freddie was all man. A true tough guy. His hands were rough and calloused. His skin was red and leathery. And that white hair made him stick out like a bug zapper.

"Hey Freddie, nice to meet you. I'm Ronnie. I talked to you in the phone about chartering a plane to Cuba. I got the money we talked about with me."

"Well hello there, Ronnie. Good to meet ya. I'm looking forward to this little adventure. I have no doubt that we can make it. Horacio is now going the opposite way."

"Well, I figured if we left right away we could make it before sundown."

"Whoa. Whoa, Cowboy. We ain't going anywhere tonight. We can leave first thing in the morning."

"Morning may be too late! She could be dead by then!!"

"Sorry, Bubba I don't have the ability to fly at night. Tomorrow morning, as early as sunrise we can take off."

Ronnie was not happy about this little development. He was under the impression that they could leave right away. He was really starting to feel the pressure. He was more worried about Kelly than anyone in his life at any time, ever.

"Alright. Morning. You sure we can leave early? I mean real early."

"Brother you hand me that cash and I can guarantee it!"

The money changed hands and Ronnie had a date. First thing tomorrow morning. Come hell or high water he'd be on that seaplane bright and early.

CHAPTER 43

The Long Walk Down a Short Drive

THE FURTHER SELENA WALKED down that dirt path, the rougher the terrain got. She wasn't a real outdoor type person. She had never hiked or went camping in her life. Christ, she was still wearing heels.

But she walked on. Walked on as the sun set. She never thought to bring a flashlight. She sure could've used one. She knew that theses woods would turn jet black in a very short period of time.

But she walked on.

It was quite a long path. She never knew it existed before and she thought she knew every dark long path in Havana.

The darkness, the terrain and the heels were a bad combo and Selena started to slip here and there. It wouldn't take long if she wasn't careful to slip and fall and really hurt herself.

As dusk settled, she looked back to where she just walked from. She could still see the main road. With the combination of all her challenges, she made the decision to walk back to the road and grab a cab back to the hospital.

CHAPTER 44

A Jerky Night.

LARRY. THE JERK. Was still on top of that plane. He had no concept of time at all. He felt like it had been dark for 4 or 5 hours and light couldn't be far off. Maybe he'd make it through the night after all.

But of course, at some point that hot sun would be back out and the Jerk would be like a piece of chicken on the grill sitting on top of that metal plane.

There had to be someone, anyone, that would make his or her way either on boat, ship or plane and see him. Rescue him. Get him off this godforsaken plane. He swore to himself that if he got out of this he would never fly again.

He was so tired. He couldn't remember the last time he slept. Was it last night or the night before? He didn't know. All he knew was that he was exhausted. He felt himself dozing. No man can fall asleep on top of a sinking plane. Can they? The Jerk thought, why not?

If you're tired enough, you could probably sleep just about anywhere. Back in Key West, Ronnie would see homeless guys sleeping on the sea wall, in the baking sun with cars zooming by.

The Jerk finally started to let nature take its course. And slowly falling asleep.

Before long, The Jerk was out like a lamp.

He fell into a deep sleep without a worry in the world.

CHAPTER 45

On the Way.

RONNIE MET FREDDIE VERY EARLY, at least very early for him. 7am on the dot. Ronnie was a little worried that Freddie was like a lot of folks in the keys and he would be on "keys time" which basically meant show up whenever the hell you wanted.

But nope. Freddie was there waiting. Funny how 10 grand can make a person on time. Ronnie should've given him half up front.

"Ronnie!" yelled Freddie. "Morning. Good to see you."

Ronnie wasn't so cheery. Not at this hour and not with his girl missing somewhere between Key West and Cuba.

"Hey Freddie. Good morning. Are we all set?"

"Yep. She's all gassed up and ready to go."

"Good! Let's do this."

Ronnie followed Freddie to the small seaplane parked a little ways away.

The first thing Ronnie thought was how damn small it was. Just the two seats in front and a small space in the back. Maybe, just maybe, Kelly could fit in that space.

Freddie waited for Ronnie to get close and opened the door for him. It was a bit of a step to get in. Ronnie thought he pulled a muscle climbing in the damn thing. Getting old blows.

Freddie then walked to the other side and hopped in easy as can be. Freddie was easily 15 years older than Ronnie and he got in the plane a whole helluva lot easier than Ronnie did. He figured he could chalk it up to repetition. Getting in and out of that thing a million times. It was still a little embarrassing.

As Freddie turned the engine over, Ronnie looked down the runway. Or what he guessed was a runway. It was more like a path. Not very long. He thought how the hell are we gonna get off the ground.

But in very short time Freddie was up to speed and they slowly got off the ground. It could not have been a more perfect day. Not a cloud in the sky. Hard to imagine Cat 5 Hurricane Horacio was out there bearing down on Jamaica.

As they leveled off a few thousand feet up, Ronnie's thoughts went back to Kelly. The good times. The many laughs. The drinks. The sex. All of it. 99.6% of the time, it was perfect. He closed his eyes. He was exhausted. This whole ordeal had taken 10 years off his life. But before he could feel too sorry for himself, he thought of what Kelly was going though. That is if she was still ... no. Ronnie wouldn't let himself think of Kelly as gone. He felt deep down in his heart that she was still alive. He had to hang onto that. Had to!

CHAPTER 46

Back to Kelly.

BY THE TIME A CAB CAME BY, Selena was surprised to say the least when it was the exact same cab she'd taken out here. The pink '57 Chevy. She hopped in and told the driver she was going back to the hospital. The driver must've thought she was nuts.

He drops her off in the middle of nowhere and now an hour later he's picking her back up. But he didn't show that he figured her out to be a nut. He greeted her kindly and off they went.

Selena hoped that Kelly would be awake. She had to tell her what she had found and then take her there. But she also knew that Kelly needed at least another night of rest at the hospital. She couldn't tell her just yet even though it was killing her not too. Selena figured whoever lived back there on that path would still be there tomorrow, so why get Kelly excited and miss another night of rest. She figured she would tell her in the morning and let her get some more shut-eye.

On the cab ride to the hospital, Selena thought of her new friend and what she had been through. From when she was a kid and was a part of this big crime story, to thinking her father had been killed, to burying her father to now. A crazy story. A good story for a book maybe.

She wondered what she would do if the shoe was on the other foot. How she would react. How she would feel if she found out her dad, who she thought was dead, showed up in another country alive and well. She thought about that for quite some time and came to the conclusion that she would be pissed. Very pissed.

And Selena wasn't the kind of person that got pissed.

She was a sweet soul. A nurse was the perfect job for her because she cared about people so much. All people. She'd work overnights and weekends whenever needed and on her spare time just to help those who needed it. Family first, then neighbors and then strangers. Whenever the call came, she'd go.

As far as family goes, Selena was a mother of 3 boys. They were all grown and out of the house and the oldest boy, Robert now had a child of his own, Jeffery. Selena was a grandmother. You'd never know it. She looked great.

She was also a very religious woman. A strong catholic. At church every Sunday no matter what. She had been to church when she was sick or depressed or tired. No matter. She'd show up to church on Sunday. Sometimes early.

She was always taking part in whatever charity drive or bake sale they were having. She was someone the church could count on and she liked being that person. Someone the church could count on. She figured if the church could count on her then she'd always be able to count on god.

Selena was not just a good woman, she had a good soul. She loved being a nurse. She'd been nursing people since she was 6 years old with her grandmother. It was fate that she would end up making a living nursing people.

And now her newest patient was Kelly. She not only cared a great deal about Kelly's health but she cared about her whole story. Her life. It was sad and she felt it. Kelly was deep down a sad, lost soul. That's how Selena felt. It's why she was working so hard to help her. She wanted to see her recover from her injuries but she also wanted her to find her Dad.

CHAPTER 47

A Hot Jerk.

THE JERK WOKE UP at the crack of dawn. On top of the plane still. He slept hard for being in the situation he was. He sat up and looked around. He was still in the ocean. The down side was he was much further out. He had drifted quite a bit during the night. He peered down into the cockpit and saw that English Bill was in fact still dead. The water was almost up to his neck now. If he were alive you'd think he would've moved by now the Jerk thought and actually chuckled to himself by that thought.

The sun would be up soon and it was going to get real hot. Real soon. Even hotter if you're sitting on top of a metal plane. What was the plan now, thought the Jerk. When the sun came up and it got hot what would he do? He dreaded the thought of getting back in the water. Sliding down the dry metal of the Cessna.

The only intact article of clothing he had were his pants. He started thinking how he could use those to stay cooler and not have to get back into the ocean. They were nice pants actually. The Jerk spared no expense when it came to clothes. But they were kind of thin. He lived in Jamaica after all. No need for heavy slacks. So if he took them off it wouldn't give him much protection from his current seat.

There really was no option when the sun came up but to slide down back into the ocean. Like a slug.

But there was still time. It wouldn't really start getting hot until maybe 10 a.m. He looked down at his Tag watch, a watch that cost him $3,000 and a watch that was holding up pretty damn good. It was a little after 7 a.m. He had some time.

Maybe the pants, which were white, could be used to flag someone down. Maybe another boat or a cruise ship or another plane. But he thought there would be little chance to see a pair of pants waving while he was in the ocean. So he put off hopping back in. He had hoped that someone would come along and see him sitting atop the wreckage and rescue him. He'd take the rescue from anyone about now. Somali pirates would even be ok, he chuckled again at the thought of Somali pirates rescuing him. "I'd end up being a slave for them and have to clean the toilets and shit," the Jerk said to himself.

As he was waiting for his salvation, he got to thinking. Thinking about his life. It really wasn't that good. He had money and girls and a great place to live but he started thinking he'd been a jerk to a lot of people over the years. Ronnie would've loved to be around for that little revelation. He would've felt so vindicated. The Jerk, Larry, thought about his success and his failures. He made a pledge then and there that if he got rescued he would change his life.

Of course a lot of guys in dire situations came to the same conclusion and then get saved and still be fucking jerks. Whether or not this Jerk could or would pull it off was a big question.

Larry the Jerk wasn't a religious man but he started to think about god. If there was one. If he was here with him now. And if he would see to it that he got rescued. "Maybe I'll go to church if I get back." And then he shrugged it off. "Nah, the place would get hit by lightning if I walked in."

After all this time thinking and talking to himself, the Jerk looked down and realized he'd killed almost a whole hour. It was around 8am now.

"What the fuck am I doing wasting time? I should be trying to come up with a plan."

But he really thought of nothing that he could do. No plan, Stan. No cigar. No idea.

So, the Jerk sat. And waited. For a miracle.

CHAPTER 48

The Blue Skies.

RONNIE AND FREDDIE WERE IN THE SKY at about 3,000 feet. Cruising. Still just a gorgeous day. Still not a cloud in the sky.

"So how long you been flying?"

"Oh shit since I was just a kid. I love it man. It's still a rush to me every time I hop in."

"Ever crash?" Ronnie immediately regretted the question. But he was tired and worried. Freddie seemed to understand.

"Not yet! And hopefully not any time soon."

"Amen!"

The two sat quiet for awhile after that little exchange. It was the only conversation they'd had since they left Key West and would be the final for some time. Finally Ronnie asked, "Where are we? Is this the straits?"

"Yep. Sure is! Pretty isn't she?"

"Yep."

Another great nugget of conversation between two men that really didn't enjoy talking too much anyway.

"How close to Cuba are we?"

"Oh just about 30 miles or so. We'll be there pretty soon."

Strike 3 on the conversation.

Ronnie decided he'd just shut up for the rest of the way.

"What the fuck?" Freddie was looking over his left shoulder and looking down. "What the fuck is that?"

"What the fuck is what? Do you see something?"

"Look down. Looks like a small plane crash or

something."

Ronnie only thought of Kelly at the time. Knew she wasn't on a plane so who cared.

And then he suddenly thought of The Jerk.

"Oh fuck me!! I paid a guy to fly to Cuba to try and find her. God I hope it's not them!"

"Well, lemme dip down a little and see if we can't get a better look."

Freddie dipped the plane to the left. He was pretty sure it was a little Cessna, but couldn't quite make it out from this altitude.

"Ho-Lee fuck!" Ronnie looked over to Freddie and started scanning the water under them at the same time.

"What?! What do you see??!"

"It's a Cessna alright. Looks like they crashed and it looks like maybe recently!"

Ronnie now had sight of the plane. It looked bad. The wings were gone and probably floated away. The fuselage was crunched pretty good. There's no way anyone survived this, Ronnie thought.

As if he was reading Ronnie's mind, Freddie said, "I can't imagine anyone surviving that!" They were now circling around the sight of the wreckage. And it didn't take long. A white flag? Of some sort.

"What the hell is that?" Ronnie asked.

"Looks like somebody is waving a flag of some sort."

Freddie dipped even lower now. As he descended towards the wreckage site, Ronnie could not believe his eyes. He could not believe that this could be happening. He thought he recognized the man there with the wreckage. On top of the wreckage?

CHAPTER 49

Could It Be?

MIRACLES DO HAPPEN. Every day, all over the world. Many people believe this, the Jerk does not. He always thought it was a bunch of shit. The whole idea of a miracle. He always thought it was coincidence or luck or something. He believed in luck.

The fact is if it wasn't for luck, the Jerk wouldn't have the life he had, not this one on top of the plane anyway, but the one he had back in Jamaica.

He started to think again about his life. He grew up in Jacksonville, Florida. Only child. Spoiled rotten. His father was a successful lawyer and his mom was a dentist. Needless to say, the Jerk had everything he wanted or needed and then some.

It was a good childhood. He loved his parents very much and they loved him back. After high school his parents assumed he would go to an Ivy League school like Cornell or Yale. He had other ideas though. He wanted some of his trust fund money now so he could go to Europe and other places. His mom and dad were pissed, but thought let him get it out of his system. Let him go. Give him the money.

So that's what happened. Larry the Jerk went to Europe. Travelled all over the country side. Had the time of his life. Party after party. At some point it was time to go home. See mom and dad.

At some point at 35,000 feet, his parents were both killed in a car accident. A drunk driver hit them and flipped their car over several times. Neither of them was wearing seat belts, because nobody wore seat belts back then. Dead on impact.

The Jerk had no idea until he got off the plane, grabbed his luggage and headed for the door. That's when he saw his cousin waiting and waving her arms. He was glad to see her. But something didn't seem right with her. Marlene had a look of sadness on her face that he hadn't seen before or ever again for that matter. She ran up to him.

"Oh Larry I'm so glad you're home!" as she hugged sobbing.

"Jesus Mar, I haven't been gone that long!"

"Larry I got some bad news. Real bad news. And I'm not sure how to tell you."

"Marlene, just tell me."

"Well, your parents were driving to the store to get groceries and other things and as they were pulling onto the highway a drunk driver came up behind them and slammed right into them." She started balling now and they hadn't even left the airport.

"So the car is wrecked I'm guessing. I was gonna use that car this summer. They couldn't wait to wreck it."

"Larry!! They're DEAD!!

That one line from another person's mouth has stuck with him ever since. They were both gone. In seconds he became an orphan.

"Dead?? Really? Holy shit. Dead!"

The jerk's head turned upwards like a cats paw. He thought he heard a sound earlier. Now he saw it too.

A plane!

A freaking plane!!

Oh God let them be able to see me, thought the Jerk.

"OVER HERE!! OVER HERE!! I'm right here!!" the Jerk yelled as he waved his white pants in the air.

He was beside himself. Was he about to be rescued? Finally?

CHAPTER 50

The News.

SELENA HAD BEEN AT THE FOOT of Kelly's bad for a few hours. Gently nodding off from time to time. Even the best nurses have to shut their eyes once in a while. She would snap awake to see Kelly in the exact same position, sleeping. Hard. Not moving at all. She was catching up on a lot of lost sleep.

As Selena sat there she wondered how she would tell Kelly. And more importantly, what if she was wrong. What if her father wasn't there? She really had no more than a hunch it was him.

She didn't want to hurt her again with the wrong information.

But she had to tell. Because what if it was? It was better to be sad than never find out. So, Selena waited. Waited for Kelly to wake.

A few hours had gone by now and Kelly for the first time seemed to move just a little bit. Selena thought she was waking up.

Kelly's eyes started to twitch and her mouth moved. She was awake. Her eyes opened and she automatically stretched. And yawned.

It took her just a few seconds for her to recognize her friend at the end of the bed, with her hand on Kelly's foot.

Selena was the last person she saw before closing her eyes and now she was the first as she woke up. That was a great deal of comfort for Kelly.

"Good morning, dear. How do you feel?"

Kelly was groggy and as she moved a little bit she was still somewhat sore. Maybe if she got out of bed she could tell better how she was. She started to do that and Selena rushed over to help.

"Go slow, dear. Go slow."

Kelly didn't think she could go anything but slow. She started to make her way to the edge of the bed and got her legs over the edge. With her hands behind her she pushed herself off the bed and for the first time in quite a while, her feet touched the cool floor.

It felt good. She felt good. She moved around a little. Walked back and forth from the bed to the doorway.

"Well, how do you feel?"

"Ya know what, I actually feel pretty good. I'm still a little tired but overall I feel good."

"Oh that's so good to hear."

Kelly was waiting for the dear that always accompanies most of Selena's sentences. She was waiting to see if she would rhyme "hear" and "dear" and was a little sad when she didn't.

"I would love to get out of here. How hard is that gonna be?"

"Not hard at all. If you feel ready, we can just check out like in a motel." Selena chuckled at her own little joke and Kelly thought it was cute. Her chuckle, not the joke.

It almost was like she forgot why she was here and where here was. It took a few minutes to let everything that had happened to her in the last few days sink in. All at once she knew why she was here. And where she was.

"I gotta get outta here. I gotta find my dad. It's why I came. I can't stop now."

Selena knew Kelly was determined. She knew all she cared about was her dad. And getting some kind of closure whether it be bad or good. Hopefully good, thought Selena. She didn't want anymore bad for Kelly.

"Listen, dear. I have to tell you something. Something about your dad. I may know where he is."

CHAPTER 51

Saving a Real Jerk.

RONNIE AND FREDDIE COULDN'T TAKE their eyes off that wreckage and off what looked like a man waving a flag. This was unbelievable.

"Well, I think we got ourselves a man in duress. We better touch down and see if we can help him."

"Do we have room? Do we have time?"

"Oh, heck yea. Won't take much time at all and we got more than enough fuel. You are ok with helping this guy, right?"

"Oh sure. Sure."

Freddie had to sort of turn around and make room for a landing. These seaplanes always impressed Ronnie. He always thought it was the coolest thing watching them land. Of course he'd never been part of a rescue with the damn thing.

Freddie got far enough out and then started back in. He was gonna land this thing pretty much right along side of the wrecked plane and the man on top.

Ronnie got to thinking how hot that damn plane was to be sitting there on top.

As Freddie got lower and closer, Ronnie almost swallowed his tongue.

"Holy shit!!"

"What's the matter Ronnie? You scared the shit out of me!"

"I know that guy! That's the guy I sent to Cuba to do the same thing we're doing now."

"You gotta be kidding me?!"

"Nope. His name is the ... er, Larry. Larry something. Can't remember his last name. But Larry, he lives in

Jamaica."

"Well his home in Jamaica is about the worst place on earth to be right now, what with Horacio and all."

Ronnie couldn't believe they just found the jerk. He thought there was a slim chance they'd make it to Cuba, so this really isn't too big a surprise now that he's thinking about it. But, shit, there he was.

Then Ronnie realized the Jerk had no shirt or pants on. God knows where his shirt was and he knew where his pants where, he was waving the god damn things like a proud flag.

Freddie was just 60 or 70 feet above now and starting getting lower and lower until ... splash. It was on the water now. Freddie was basically driving on the water now and getting close to the Jerk.

Ronnie stuck his head out of the side door and yelled, "Larry!! What the fuck?!!"

"Holy fuck!! Ronnie??"

"Oh my god what the hell happened? Where's Bill??"

"Bill's in the same place he was when we left Jamaica. Behind the wheel."

That's when Ronnie could get a good view of the cockpit and saw English Bill sitting "behind the wheel" very much dead. Red all over his shirt and face. Dry sticky red. It looked as if he took an airplane window to the face.

"Holy crap!" Freddie yelled. He's probably never seen another pilot dead like this before.

As they sidled up to the little plane, Ronnie was close enough to the Jerk where he could reach out his hand and touch him.

"Gimme your hand!"

"I can't quite reach, come a little closer!"

What a jerk. Freddie couldn't come any closer if he wanted to. His plane and the wrecked plane were almost touching side by side.

"You're gonna have to jump in and swim over to us. I

can help you on once you get over here. Slid down the side and swim over!"

Larry thought Ronnie was a jerk this time. The whole idea of sliding down a hot dry piece of metal made the Jerk think Ronnie had never played on a slide in the park during a hot summer when he was a kid.

"Easier said than done!"

"Well it's either that or we leave your ass here! How bout that?!"

The Jerk just realized he didn't like Ronnie very much.

"I'm coming. I'm coming!"

Ronnie watched the almost comical sight of the Jerk trying to slowly slide down the side of this plane. Almost a skip and a slide. Any other circumstances and this would've been fucking hilarious.

As the Jerk hit the water, even though the water was around 84 degrees, Ronnie could hear a very loud sigh of relief to be off that hot roof.

The Jerk started to half walk/swim/wade towards Ronnie and Freddie. This whole time Freddie was quiet. He really couldn't stop looking at the very dead English bill.

"Holy shit, Ronnie. I thought I was gonna fucking die out here!" the Jerk yelled as he waded over.

Ronnie reached out his hand and easily pulled him in. The Jerk looked like a Florida Lobster. Red as can be. His face was beat red and so was the rest of him and there was nothing left to the imagination. The only thing the Jerk was now wearing was a nice pair of shoes and a pair of silk boxers.

As the Jerk sat down and settled in to that tiny space in the back, Ronnie looked back and smiled, "You're quite a sight, man."

"I've been through hell, man. There's a ton of sharks and shit out here!"

"I bet. Well, we got you now. You're safe."

Freddie also turned around and introduced himself to the Jerk.

"Freddie it's damn nice to meet you! Thanks for stopping by."

Ronnie never knew the Jerk to be funny, but in the last 5 minutes anyway he was pretty damn funny. Freddie threw a towel to the back "seat" and said, "Dry off a little."

"I got some clothes back there. A pair of shorts and a shirt anyway. They should fit ya."

"Oh thanks so much."

Ronnie turned back around and Freddie started making his way back out and up. Within a few minutes all three men were in the sky.

"So where are you going? Have you been to Cuba yet? Any luck?"

"We were on our way there when we saw you. I'm still hoping we can land safely in Cuba and find Kelly still. I'm hoping we're not too late!"

The Jerk sat back in his seat and dried off and then put Freddie's shirt and shorts on. He was shaking a little bit. Most likely a little shock from the trauma of it all.

"What about English Bill?" asked Larry.

"I'm about to call in the coordinates to the coast guard. They'll grab him up and take him back."

"Ok."

At that moment all 3 men became uncomfortably quiet. What could be said?

They were 30 minutes out of Cuba and they're 2 planes and 1 life into this trip that might not amount to a steaming pile of shit.

CHAPTER 52

Finding Nemo.

KELLY SAT BACK DOWN on the bed hard. "What do you know?!"

"Well, I got to thinking about a man who lived down a path that was from America. He'd been here for many years. So I took a cab to where I'd heard this man was. I started walking down the path but it got dark and too dangerous so I came back here to check on you."

"Fucking A! Let's go back! Do you remember where it was??!!"

"Yes, dear. I sure do."

As Kelly dressed she got more and more excited. This could be it! She could be hugging her father in just a short amount of time. Or kicking him in the nuts first and then hugging him.

It had been a long few days for Kelly. She thought about her little Island home in Key West. How much she missed it. All of it. The big old houses and trees. The Spanish limes. The hibiscus flowers. Even the conch trains and trolleys that inundated her neighborhood daily with silly stories about the history of Key West. If only they knew the real stories, Kelly thought.

She missed Ronnie most of all. Missed him real bad. She'd known for a long time that she was in love with him. She would rather be with him in that apartment than anywhere else in the world.

She had to put it all out her mind. She had a job to do here in Cuba and she had every intention of carrying it out. She had to accomplish this, no matter the consequences or how this would turn out.

She figured there were only a couple ways this could go.

1) He would deny the whole thing.

2) He would admit the whole thing.

That's it. The only two ways this could end.

She had hoped more than anything that he would choose number 2. She wanted a Dad. Her dad. She wanted him back. She never really got over him dying. When her mom died, that was tough, but losing dad, especially the way she did, was far harder. She mourned more for her dad than her mom.

Kelly was dressed and checked out and walking out of the hospital with her new best friend, Selena. She loved Selena. Hoped she would come back to key west with her. Then again maybe Kelly would stay here. It was a pretty amazing place.

"We'll catch a cab and head over there. It's going to be about a 20 minute ride."

It was if Selena was preparing Kelly for a test.

"Ok. I just wanna get there."

"I know, dear. I want this to be perfect for you."

"Selena, I love you for helping me while I've been here. And going as far as you did to find my father."

"Well, I just felt so bad about telling you the wrong man died. I had to do something. I spent some time around the neighborhood asking about your father. It took a long time and a lot of questions to finally get someone who knew something. But when I found them, they sang like a hummingbird."

"I'm just so excited. And mad." Kelly said as they climbed into another '57 Chevy, this one teal colored.

"Why mad?"

"Because of what he put my whole family through. Especially my Mom."

"Honey, you have to let that go. God is brining you

two together now for some reason. I'm sure it's not to fight or bring up the past. I'm sure god is bringing you together in the name of love."

Oh, good grief, Kelly thought. Selena was a little too positive. In real life when someone hurts you, you dream about hurting them back. Maybe that was just Kelly.

"Yea maybe you're right, Selena. I hope you're right."

CHAPTER 53

Welcome to Cuba.

AS FREDDIE, RONNIE, AND THE JERK taxied into Havana Harbor, they all had separate fears. Freddie was afraid someone would fuck with his plane. The Jerk was afraid of just being in a foreign country like Cuba. And Ronnie was afraid he'd never see Kelly again.

As they hopped off, the Cuban police where right there. The same cops that roughed up Kelly.

"Oh Jesus, here they come!" The Jerk was already terrified.

"Big deal. They ain't nothing to worry about. I've been here a hundred times. I know all these fuckers with badges."

Within a few minutes, Freddie stood on the harbor just chatting with the cops. It looked like he did indeed know them. Ronnie and the Jerk stayed back. And waited. Nervously.

"Come on guys, let's go. We're in!"

Ronnie didn't hesitate, but the Jerk did. He had no interest of going any further and either did Freddie. The Jerk was scared but Freddie just wanted to keep the plane safe.

"Ronnie, this is Corporal Melendez. He's sort of the chief of police in Havana. A good guy. Corporal meet Ronnie. He's a famous American author!"

"Good to meet you, Mr. Ronnie. What is your business in Cuba?"

Ronnie thought for a second how to answer that question. Did he really want to tell the police chief that he was here to find his girlfriend?

"I'm here as a journalist. I write a column for the Times and I want to do a piece about tourism here."

The corporal looked Ronnie over. He looked like the journalist type. Sort of prim and proper.

If Ronnie knew that this cop thought he was prim and proper he would fall down laughing and not get up for an hour.

"What do you think, Mr. Freddie? Should I let him in?"

Now it was Freddie's turn to look Ronnie over with a smile.

"Yea, he's a good guy. Just writing an article for the times."

It was if Freddie said that to make himself believe it. He knew it was bullshit, but he still had 10 grand and he had Ronnie to thank for it.

Ronnie started thinking: If Freddie knew these cops and they were the cops in Havana, maybe they would have some idea where Kelly might be.

"Hey Freddie, ask them about Kelly. Maybe they know something."

"Oh yea right. Hey Miguel, do you know anything about a young lady that came here about 2 or 3 days ago? White, thin, brownish hair. From Key West?"

The look that came over Miguel's face was a mix of fear and embarrassment. Ronnie immediately picked up on it but didn't say anything. If these pricks did something with Kelly or hurt her, he would kill em all, he thought.

"White girl, from key west. Doesn't ring a bell."

"Think about it, it was just 2 days ago, man," said Ronnie a little pissy.

Miguel did not take kindly to Ronnie's attitude. "Well, *man*, we have a lot of people that come here from all over the world, not just key west."

Ronnie thought he just fucked up everything. If

he's pissed off the chief, or whatever he was, he'd be sunk finding Kelly. He needed the cops. Besides Ronnie brought a ton of cash with him for just this kind of challenge. He had always heard cops in places like Cuba could be bought. Ronnie was about to find out. He had around 50 Grand in a suitcase in the plane. No clothes, just money.

"Forgive me. I'm a little upset about my missing girlfriend. We think she may be here in this beautiful country of yours."

"I understand and I accept your apology. Maybe we could help. Even though our resources are very limited."

Bingo! Ronnie had him.

"Well I have significant resources. Maybe we can help each other out."

The chief stopped looking at his feet and looked directly into Ronnie's eyes.

"What does that mean, you have significant resources?"

"Well, I've made a very good life for myself and have been very successful."

"I'm sorry. I don't quite understand."

"I have a lot of fucking money!" Ronnie blurted that one out and regretted it almost instantly. But he has such a low tolerance for stupidity. Always has.

The chief burst out laughing.

"I know exactly what you're talking about. Maybe we should go to my office and chat. See if something can't be worked out and maybe if we're lucky we'll find your girlfriend."

Ronnie felt kind of dirty. Like when you've been mowing the lawn in the hot 90 degree sun and come in the house and you're filthy and sweaty and you just want to take a shower before you do anything. Even sit down.

Yep. THAT feeling.

That's how Ronnie felt right now. And he could taste the disgust. He wanted a shower and to brush his teeth all of a sudden in the worst way.

"Well let's go see your office!"

CHAPTER 54

Another Cab Ride.

SELENA AND KELLY HAD MADE IT to the other side of Havana. They were just a quick 5-minute walk to that path Selena had already been on. A path that may lead to much more than just leaves and trees. Maybe Frank(ie) Alvarez.

"Are you ok to walk, dear?"

"Yes ma'am I sure am!" Kelly was ready. Emotionally and even physically. She was ready to walk down that path to her past and see the man who is her dad, maybe, today.

She thought about what she would do. What she would say. She just knew all the shit that she wanted to say she never would. She would probably just hug him and cry. Kind of like when you meet a big time politician and you're going to tell him off good. Give him a piece of your mind. And then when you meet him you're just dumbfounded or star struck. That's probably how it would go if she saw her Dad today.

They began to walk that 5 minutes to the path. What Kelly was feeling was hard to describe. Anxiety for sure. A little bit of panic even. She sort of felt like this was a dream. A fuzzy dream and she wasn't even in it. It was like looking at someone else's dream. It was very bizarre.

It had been a long long time since she saw her father. She thought about the beautiful casket. Wondering now what was in there. Was it empty? Was it filled with rocks? The whole idea of the closed casket was because he had been riddled with bullets. And of course now she knew that couldn't have been the case.

It was a very quiet 5-minute walk. Kelly was anxious and nervous and Selena was also. Selena felt like if this wasn't her father, she wouldn't be able to face Kelly. That would mean she tortured her twice. She wouldn't be able to live with herself. She also wanted this to be her dad so she could move on with her life and find some peace and love.

The 5 minutes actually went by pretty quick. Selena stopped in her tracks and just pointed. At first Kelly didn't see what she was pointing at. Then after about 10 seconds she saw.

It was a tiny path maybe the width of a very small car. If you didn't know it was there, you'd never give it a second thought. Maybe you wouldn't even see it. There were trees and brush all around it. Almost hiding it. It was the kind of path that you loved to go exploring down when you were 12 years old. You'd go because it was spooky and the unknown was down that path. It was still sort of that way for Kelly now. It wasn't so much spooky but certainly it was unknown.

They stood now at the entrance to that path. Neither took a step and neither said a word. They both just looked.

There were no excuses. There was no reason they wouldn't or shouldn't walk down that path, but still they didn't move. Kelly started to think, what if the reason he left was me? She thought, what if all he wanted to do was to get away from me and the family. Why else would he go to such lengths as he did?

"Well, I guess this is it, Selena. You don't have to go down there with me, just finding this was way more than you had to do."

"Oh, Kelly" (she was surprised to hear her use her name instead of Dear), "I want to go with you. To be with you either way."

Kelly couldn't help but think what a great friend she had found in Selena. She had always been blessed with great people in her life. In her hardest days, when she got into trouble or was just down on her luck, she always had people that believed in her and stuck by her and loved her. Blessed for sure.

"Selena, I really love you for being here with me. I would never have come this close without you."

Selena smiled and winked at Kelly.

But the time for smiles and winks and "I love you" was over. The time to take those first steps down that path was now. Kelly looked down the path first. It was kind of spooky after all. It was overgrown with thick brush. It looked very hilly and rocky too. It actually looked like it might be a tough walk.

Kelly took a look behind her and above her as if to say this is it. No going back.

She took a deep breath and she took that first step.

CHAPTER 55

Office Visit.

HERE RONNIE SAT, IN CUBA, inside a police station and jail, in the chief's office. How he found himself here sort of blew his mind. If you had asked him 20 years ago, or even 10 years ago, or even a week ago that this is where he'd be, he'd tell you to lay off the crack.

Freddie decided to stay behind to keep an eye on the plane and the Jerk stayed behind because he was a pussy. It was just Ronnie, the chief and 4 other Cuban cops. It was a little intimidating. Anything could happen and Ronnie would never be seen again. What would anyone do? The cops could say anything and what could you or anyone do? Nothing is the answer.

"Do you like cigars?" asked the chief Miguel.

"As a matter of fact I do."

"Well you are in Cuba after all. Home to the best tobacco and the best cigars anywhere. People from all over the world desire our cigars."

"I am aware of this," said Ronnie

At this point, the chief Miguel reached into a drawer and pulled out a beautiful wooden box. It looked like it was a hundred years old. He dropped it on the desk way harder than Ronnie thought he should have.

"These are those cigars that people all over the world desire."

Miguel pulled one out and handed it to Ronnie over the desk.

Ronnie had never been a fan of Cuban cigars but now as he lit and smoked this one, he thought maybe every other cigar he smoked that people told him were Cubans could in fact not have been real Cubans.

This was a cigar. The finest thing Ronnie had ever smoked. And he smoked a lot of things in his life. The experience of sitting in a Cuban police station and smoking a Cuban cigar with the Cuban police chief who's name was Miguel was surreal. But Ronnie puffed. He was truly taking in this moment. He had for at least a little bit forgotten about Kelly. About what he was doing here. It almost felt like a vacation.

"So Mr. Ronnie, it would seem that you may have a problem that I can help you with is that right?"

"I think you can absolutely help me. I'm looking for my girlfriend, Kelly Alvarez. She's here in Cuba, I think, I hope. She's looking for her father who faked his death and abandoned her many years ago. She may be lost or hurt or dead. But I need to find her and then find her father."

Miguel leaned back in his large leather chair like Boss Hog. He took a deep draw on his cigar. He looked up at the dingy ceiling. Took a deep contemplative sigh and then looked right at Ronnie.

"Mr. Ronnie, I'll be honest with you. We don't much care for Americans here. We like the idea of America but we would rather do without all of you. So when someone like you comes here looking for help, we don't jump very high to help."

Ronnie was feeling the drain of losing Kelly, the trip. He was exhausted. He leaned in and put his forearms on the Chief's desk.

"Miguel, I'll be honest with you. I could give a fuck what you think about America. I'm not a big fan of Cubans. So as long as we understand that, we can probably do business. I have more money in my suitcase than this town has in the bank. So let's cut with the bullshit and get down to business, because whether you like me or not, or don't like where I'm from doesn't make one fuck of a difference. This is business and nobody likes anybody they do business with. Understand where I'm coming from?"

Miguel took another lean in the leather chair. This time putting one foot on the desk. He looked at Ronnie for a long time. Ronnie looked right back. Miguel was the first to crack. He smiled. A big toothy smile.

"You might be the first American I've ever liked!!"

Miguel and the other 4 cops laughed hard.

Ronnie just sat there. Stone cold.

"Excuse me, Miguel, if I don't think any of this is funny. My life is not a joke. My girl is not a joke. The joke is here. This place. This fucking place!"

"Mr. Ronnie, excuse me, but this place you speak of is not a joke at all. You came here. Your girl came here. Your girl's father came here."

"Yes and lots of Cubans come to my country as well. Listen, are we gonna fuck around or are we gonna do business? Did you bring me here to laugh at or something else?"

"No, No, we want to do business. Forgive our laughter. It is, how you say, an inside joke. What exactly do you want from us, Mr. Ronnie?"

"I told you already. I need to find Kelly first and then maybe her father. I'd rather just take her and get the fuck back home."

"I see. And you are willing to pay for the full and complete cooperation and service of the Havana police department?"

"I am. Name your price?"

Miguel took a long pause as if to really think this over, but Ronnie believed he already had the number in mind.

"One million US dollars."

Miguel said it like he was ordering a sandwich. No emotion and he was dead serious.

Ronnie, though, wasn't in the mood to screw around.

"Are you out of your fucking mind?! I mean who do you think you're dealing with here, some asshole who's never been off an island before!" He was pissed. The very idea of a million dollars was ridiculous.

"Relax, Mr. Ronnie, that was just the starting point. This is a little negotiation."

"Alright, fine. Here's my little negotiation. I'll give you $50,000 and not a penny more. Take it or leave it. I don't give a shit about your help. I will spread my money all over this place and find what I need with or without you. Either you get the whole 50K or I'll spread it around to 100 villagers. The result will be the same."

Ronnie had slammed the ball back in Miguel's face. It felt good too. For Ronnie, that is. He had no intention of letting these fuckers screw him out of a million dollars.

Miguel was looking at the 4 other cops. He knew Ronnie was right. In a city where a lot of poor people live the kind of money Ronnie was talking about throwing around would get him a tremendous amount of help. He'd probably find her quicker doing it that way.

"We will agree to an initial payment of your $50,000, but reserve the right to another $50,000 if we incur great stress or loss. We know of this man you speak and he has and maybe still is wrapped up with some very dangerous people. We have to protect ourselves and our families."

Ronnie thought about this for a minute. He had the money with him, but that was all he brought in that suitcase. The look on the bankers face back in Key

West when he went in and withdrew 100 grand was one of the best things Ronnie had ever seen. He wasn't printing his own money but Ronnie was very wealthy. Some put his wealth at around 30 or 40 million dollars.

But even for someone with that kind of money, 100 grand was a big hit. The banker called Ronnie into his office. The bankers name was Jim Hail. Jim was a good guy. A local who'd been on the island a long time. He was very active in the community. A fisherman and a charter captain on the side. He was crazy about wildlife and the environment. He had an awesome dog as a pet and even a damn bird that would go fishing with him. Hell, Jim was even a bee keeper. Pretty cool guy.

Jim sat down with Ronnie and tried to reason with him.

"Ronnie this is a shit ton of money. I mean, if you want it, you got it, but Christ man ... "

"Jim, don't worry about it man. I haven't lost my marbles or anything, I just am making a large purchase and need the money up front."

"I mean that's a pretty big damn down payment!"

"Jim, I'm not buying a house or making a big purchase. I just need the money for some personal shit. When it's all said and done I'll fill you in, but for right now I just need your cute little teller out there to go into the vault and fill up my pretty suitcase with a thousand-hundred-dollar bills."

"Well, we're definitely going to do it, I just want to make sure you didn't have a head injury or something like that. That's a lot of damn money. "

"Tell me about it. Can I get my case filled now? Or do you want to call a psychologist in to examine me?"

"I have the shrink on speed dial for when you come in. I never know what the hell you're gonna ask for!"

Ronnie and Jim laughed.

If it was anyone else, Ronnie would have to tell him to mind his fucking business, but he and Hail had been friends for over a decade. He was just doing his job as a banker and friend.

So Ronnie knew he had a hundred grand on him. He had every intention on coming back home with most of it still in that pretty little suitcase. This whole experience was costing him a small fortune, and he wasn't about to call Jim Hail and ask him to wire another $900,000 to Cuba!

"Alright, I'll do 50 grand now and if shit gets bad I'll throw in the other 50, but only if shit goes bad. You're not getting the whole 100 grand just for fun."

Miguel looked at the other cops. Clearly these were guys he trusted and respected.

One of the cops nodded and smirked back to Miguel.

"Ok, we have a deal." Miguel reached out his hand and Ronnie grabbed it.

He just made a 100-thousand-dollar Cuban deal to find Kelly.

CHAPTER 56

The First Step Is a Doozy.

"YOU DON'T HAVE TO WALK down here with me, Selena. You've done enough."

"As your personal nurse I have to walk in with you just to make sure you're healthy."

This made Kelly laugh for the first time in 3 days. They both smiled at each other and holding hands as friends do, they took the first step together.

It was still early morning so there was plenty of light leading the way. This path did seem to go on and on infinity. As they entered Kelly noticed what Selena had already discovered. It was sort of a tricky path. Plenty of rocks and brush crossing the path like chickens in Key West crossing the street. Of course chickens in Key West are the only ones who know how to use the crosswalks.

Kelly realized she was more sore than she was letting on. The adrenaline made her forget but now that they were actually making the trek, she felt every inch of that attack. Her legs were sore, her ribs and chest and her back. All sore. She of course would never tell Selena that. Ever.

As they walked and crisscrossed all the rocks and branches and trees and brush, it was truly like an obstacle course, Kelly noticed that Selena was humming amazing grace. That was one of Kelly's favorites and it made her feel so much more comfortable.

They had been walking for about 30 minutes when they stopped dead in their tracks. It was a noticeable smell of something cooking. It was an unrecognizable smell, but whatever it was it was for lunch they guessed.

"What the hell is that?" Kelly asked Selena.

"I'm not sure. It smells like some kind of meat, but I don't know."

Some kind of meat isn't the most pleasing sentence in the world. It's not what you want to hear when you ask what's the special at a restaurant and the waitress says, "Oh, some kind of meat."

After a quick pause they marched on. The walk was getting a little tiring. It was getting much rockier and slippery. Both of the women had slipped a few times each time to be balanced by the other. It was likely that if they didn't have each other, and were alone, they both would have fallen by now. At least once.

Kelly's mind began to drift back to her childhood in Key West. What an amazing place to grow up. She remembered always being so proud of her Dad. She went practically everywhere with him. On Sunday, they'd take a ride around the island in his big beige Pontiac. Kelly loved that car. Loved the smell of Dad, leather and gasoline. Dad always smelled good. He was an old spice man.

Kelly thought back when Dad and Mom would get gussied up for a night out, which didn't happen often, and Dad would come down the stairs after showering and shaving and he would come up behind Kelly while she was sitting in the lounger and very lightly tap her cheeks. She would smell that old spice on his hands. She loved that. She could still feel his hands on her face and still smell that old spice.

Old Spice, as crazy as it sounds, was what drew Kelly to Ronnie. He was also an old spice man. Maybe there is some truth to a girl wanting to marry someone like her dad.

There were so many good memories like that. Sometimes her father could be such a sweet man and do the sweetest things for her. And of course there where daddy's down days. His dark days. The days when daddy just wasn't himself.

In the 1800's they would've diagnosed him with "melancholy", today they diagnose it as depression. Whatever you want to call it, he had it. Some days you couldn't do anything right. He would snap at the slightest thing.

He was always a complicated man. He had many layers like an onion. Always thinking deeply. Always concerned about one thing or another. But he was one of the most well-liked and respected men on the island. The driveway always had extra cars in it. People would come to her daddy for advice or help with their problems and he would always have an answer. He would listen very carefully and then sit back in his recliner and think while looking at the ceiling. His advice would always start with, "Ya know what I think ...?"

Men always left the house in a better place than when they arrived. Her dad could give the best advice. He certainly gave her some great advice along the way. He was so smart.

§

Kelly felt like they had to be at least 3/4 of the way down this path. The strange part was the further down the path they walked, the darker it got. There where so many trees and brush it almost completely blocked out the day.

They continued. They looked at each other and had the same face. One of worry and excitement. It was hard to tell who was more of both. Selena just wanted it to be her dad and so did Kelly. She been through a helluva lot in the last few days and now she was so close. So very close. She almost wanted to run the rest of the way down the path. But she was too afraid and too sore.

Selena was riddled with guilt still for telling Kelly about a man who died who she thought was Frank Alvarez but wasn't. She remembered Kelly's face when she learned that, nope. Wrong guy. It was awful.

"Dear, I just want to say again how sorry I am for mixing up your father with that other man. I just feel so awful about that."

"Selena, I don't want you to ever worry about that again. It was an honest mistake and I've already forgotten about. So please don't worry about that. You've done so much for me. I just love you."

Kelly reached over and gave Selena a little peck on the cheek. Selena thought that was so sweet of her. She really did care about Kelly a great deal. In just a very short time, Selena loved Kelly. She loved how tough she was. She loved how tenacious she was. She loved that Kelly was a fighter and went after what she wanted. Selena wasn't so sure she could've done what Kelly had done. She was certain she wasn't strong enough for that.

Kelly truly loved Selena. When someone saves you and then spends time caring for you, it's easy to love that person. But sometimes after the doctoring up, the doctor goes away and that's that. But Selena stayed. She sat at the bedside and held Kelly's hand. She quietly prayed on the foot of the bed as Kelly drifted in and out of sleep. Kelly heard her praying. She cleaned Kelly's face and kept her temperature down with cool towels. Everything you could imagine someone doing for you after something like that had happened, Selena did. And then some. Not to mention spending her own time to investigate and find this path. Selena was one in a million and Kelly could only see them become closer over the years.

Kelly was shaken out of her daydreams. The smell of food cooking and a camp became so strong now it felt like it was only 50 or so yards ahead. But the path was so thick with forest, you still couldn't see anything.

Kelly went from being frustrated to terrified in less time it takes to heat up a cup of coffee in the microwave. She now was close enough she could see the building, and the fire burning, and ...

... a man.

CHAPTER 57

Let's Make a Deal.

RONNIE AND MIGUEL HEADED OUT into the streets of Havana. It was a damn hot day. Like Key West, which wasn't so pleasant there either this time of year. It was actually a little hotter here. In summertime Key West it would rarely get too far above 90 degrees, but in Cuba they would often reach 100 degrees, or more. Brutal.

As they stumbled into the sunlight from that very dark or some would say shady police station, Ronnie had not one clue where they were going and he wondered strongly if Miguel did either.

"Do you have any idea where you're going?"

"I do. We need to find a White American who's been hiding in Havana for decades, right? How stupid do you think we are here, Mr. Ronnie? Do you think we notice nothing?"

Ronnie was actually a little surprised by that answer. Miguel made it sound like he knew exactly where Kelly's father was and everything about him.

"I'm sorry, man. I didn't mean to offend you. I just can't imagine where we go from here."

"Isn't that why you paid me $100,000?!"

"Yea, $50,000. And yes you are the leader on this little expedition. I'm sorry. Lead on!"

Ronnie honestly could give a shit about finding Frank. His only goal was finding Kelly and bringing her home with him, with or without Frank.

There was a small white police car outside the station that was clearly only going to hold Ronnie and Miguel. They crammed in and Miguel turned the key.

The small car cranked and cranked and cranked and finally fired. Miguel threw it in gear and down the road they went.

"Jesus Christ! Can it be any hotter? I don't suppose this little shit box has air conditioning does it?"

"You like to complain a lot don't you? Americans are soft. There's much we don't have here and are fine with it."

"Whatever. I'm just saying ... a little AC wouldn't kill ya."

Miguel ignored Ronnie's whining and drove on. Down the road they went. Ronnie thought about Kelly again. She'd been on his mind and nothing else for the last 3 days. He can't believe love snuck up on him, like love often does.

The two men, one who was hot and one who didn't care, made their way through the center of Havana and kept driving right through town. Ronnie was surprised at how fast it didn't feel like downtown anymore. They had only driven for maybe 10 minutes and it seemed much more green and tropical and jungly than 10 minutes prior.

As they went around one particularly sharp corner, Miguel slowed down. And then stopped.

"What's this? Where are we?" For a second Ronnie thought Miguel was going to fondle him or something. It was so weird that they stopped all of a sudden with zero warning.

"His camp is back there. Down that path. He's been there for years. Down that path is where you'll find the man you're looking for. I'll wait here."

So that's it, Ronnie thought. And then out loud, "So that's it? I'm just supposed to believe you, get out of the car god knows where and walk down a dingy dark path where a bear will eat me?"

"First of all, there are no bears in Cuba. There really is no dangerous wildlife here. Have a little trust in me. I'm a police officer."

Neither one of them could keep a straight face with that one.

"Alright, fucker. I'll take the bait. I'll walk down this little path. But I swear to Christ if it's not what you say it is, I will spend every dime I have and buy this whole fucking island just to see you rot in jail!"

"Jesus, Mr. Ronnie. You're an angry man. I'll be waiting right here."

Ronnie stepped out of the car. He looked around. It was a beautiful place. A beautiful country. Fucking hot as hell, but beautiful. He looked at the entrance to the path. Then he looked down the path. It was dark and freaking spooky.

"Man, this better not kill me," he said out loud to himself and then smirked.

Ronnie took his first step down the path Kelly had already started on.

CHAPTER 58

Only One Leg.

AS KELLY AND SELENA CONTINUED their walk and continued to follow their noses, it got darker and darker. You could tell it was still daytime, but much much darker if that made any sense.

Just when they both were extremely tired of walking over rocks, branches, and roots, the path started to open up. There was light at the end of the tunnel, just like they always say!

The building or Shack really was visible for the first time. There indeed was a fire going and now she heard someone grumbling and talking, angrily it sounded. Or maybe just grumpily.

They slowed down to almost nothing. Surprised that this was it. Nervous in their bellies at what they were about to discover. This was it! After all these years, Kelly was going to be reunited with her father that she buried decades ago.

They looked at each other and Kelly kind of shrugged as if to say, Well, This is it. C'mon.

But they didn't take one more step. As the twigs snapped behind them, it was too late. They both spun around hard to see a disgusting man holding a gun to their faces.

He was filthy. He looked like he hadn't had a bath in 10 years. His hair was white and stringy and he had a long beard that looked like it hadn't been trimmed since the last time he took a bath. The teeth he did have were brown and decaying. His face was covered in dirt and filth. He was only wearing an old wife beater and a pair of boxers. What's shocking was they didn't notice the smell sooner. He smelled like something right out of the shit factory.

Kelly only had a second to notice, but she noticed his boxers pretty clearly. They hung near the handles of his crutches. But something was missing. There was one leg hole in the boxers not being used. Because he only had one leg!

Kelly and Selena let out a shriek as they spun around and saw this gruesome looking beast-man.

"Who the fuck are you and what do ya want?"

Neither woman had it in her to respond at first. They were terrified.

"WELL?! Answer me before I put a round in both of your bellies!"

"My name is Kelly and this is Selena. We're looking for my dad. We were told he lived here!"

Kelly was looking at this beast-man standing in front of her. How could anyone confuse this disgusting human for her Daddy? There was no way this was Frank Alvarez. Not possible, she thought.

"Kelly who?"

"Alvarez. I was told my dad Frank Alvarez was living here."

There was a long pause. The gun came down and the look in this man's face changed. Softened just a bit.

He seemed to recognize something. Someone. Something in this man's head clicked. Kelly couldn't tell what was happening but he had changed in just a second or two. "Kelly? My Kelly? From Key West? Oh my god! Kelly!"

Neither woman knew what to do. Kelly wasn't about to go hug this disgusting man. And there was no way, as she'd already thought, that this man was her father anyway.

"Who are you?" Kelly asked.

"I'm exactly who you're looking for."

"Dad???"

"It's been a long time, kiddo. You look great."

Kelly was completely thrilled that she had finally found her dad, but he was so disgusting he was like bug repellent and Kelly was a fly. She had no intention of touching him.

Her Dad sensed his own grotesqueness and instead of a long over due hug, he said, "Why don't we go over and sit down."

Kelly followed her Dad as he hopped along the way to the center of his camp. They sat down on two old huge logs. Selena and Kelly on one and Dad on the other.

Selena was as quiet as a church mouse the whole time. Could you imagine being the third wheel at a time like this?

Kelly and her dad just stared at each other for the longest time. He looked at her with loving eyes and happiness. She looked at him with disgust and revulsion. Her Dad broke the silence with repetition, "You look good, kiddo. It's been a long time."

"Dad, I, I, don't even know where to start."

She couldn't help feeling that this was not her dad. He just looked so old and thin and gross. Her Dad was so young and vibrant and ... well, clean. The smell coming off him was definitely not old spice, just gross old man, maybe.

"Let's start at the beginning," her Dad said.

Suddenly all those years of hurt and anger bubbled to the surface and she blurted out, "Why the fuck did you do this to me and mom and everyone else??!!!"

CHAPTER 59

The Light at the ...

RONNIE WAS SLOWLY MAKING his way down the path. This was such bullshit. All this aggravation and money for what? Every time he slipped on a rock or tripped over a branch he would yell, "FUCK! Are you kidding me??!!"

He wished he were back in his Key West pad. Drinking a sour. He wished he were single. That it was just him and his dogs. That he was reclined in his comfy chair watching mind numbing TV. Sitting in his cool little apartment, that was actually cool. Because a civilized human being had fucking air conditioning, he thought.

He continued to walk, but slower. It was a tricky walk for sure. He had to move slower. It was after all getting darker on this path, even though it was just a little after Noon. He was surprised by how dark it was getting. It was almost impossible to see the sun at this point.

Why would anyone want to live back here? To live like this, Ronnie thought. No matter the circumstances he would never live this way. Shit, he had to have money, Ronnie thought. Why not live in a hotel or an apartment or buy a house, anything but live like this. Animals don't even like it out here, he thought.

As he continued to walk and hopefully get closer to the end, he started to smell what he thought was a fire of some sort. A campfire? He wasn't sure, but he figured he had to be coming to the end. "Shit, maybe somebody really does live back here like a fucking rat," Ronnie said out loud to no one in particular.

It was then that Ronnie noticed the light. The light at the end of the tunnel? No. The light at the other end of this God forsaken path. He'd been walking at least 30 minutes and it's been the longest 30 minutes of his life.

He smelled the smoke even more now. But it was a different kind of smoke that he didn't recognize. It didn't smell like anything cooking necessarily, it just smelled odd. Different.

Ronnie continued walking. He was thinking now what he would say to the scumbag who calls himself Kelly's father, if that was his little campfire burning.

What kind of man would do that to his family? he thought. His wife, his kids, his friends. All of them were at his funeral for Christ sake.

Ronnie loathed this man he had never met. Hated him for what he has done to Kelly. Hated him for bringing Kelly here and putting her life in danger. Hated him for making Ronnie come here. Making him spend a small fortune. It wasn't just about the money to Ronnie, but fuck he lost a ton of it. He did what he did for a girl that means an awful lot to him. That's the end of the story there. He did it for love? Maybe. Just maybe.

Ronnie had spent so much time walking and thinking and watching where he was going he didn't realize the path ended in about 20 yards.

It became obvious to him now that he heard voices. At least two. One he didn't know but one he knew very well. It was a woman's voice. And she was pissed. Yelling.

Ronnie knew that voice because he had seen and heard her yelling. He knew what she sounded like when she was pissed. She had yelled at him that way a few times.

There was no doubt in his mind who that voice belonged to, it was

KELLY!

CHAPTER 60

Old Fucker.

KELLY SAT ACROSS FROM HER FATHER. Staring at him. How disgusting he was. What he had become. She didn't know what to expect but it sure as hell wasn't this. This awful looking and smelling human being missing a leg that was sitting in front of her. Smiling. He was smiling.

"What the fuck are you smiling about? Do you have any idea what you put me and mom and everyone else through?! We buried you! We lost a lifetime with you. You put us through fucking hell!!! How dare you sit there and fucking smile at me! I feel like taking a rock and smashing your god damn face with it!"

It was all coming out and her father knew it. He let her go. He knew it was a part of what she had to do. He didn't like it, but he had no right to interrupt her. Or to yell back or what, send her to her room?! Those days were long gone.

She hated what he had done to her and his family and friends.

"You old fucker! I hate you for what you've done to us. I hate you for being the furthest thing from what I thought you were. My dad would've never done this to us. That's what I thought at least."

She was still yelling. Loudly. If there were any bears here, she would've woken them all up by now. She was yelling so loudly there was a better than good chance people out on the road at the start of the path may have heard her. She could've cared less. She was letting over 20 years of pain out. 20 years of hurt. Of therapy. Of people mocking her behind her back and telling stories and whispering around her.

This old fucker, this disgusting old fucker had ruined her life. Changed it forever.

Selena still had not said a word. This was more colorful language than she ever wanted to hear, but she also knew this was part of the process. She had to get it out.

As Kelly was about to tear into her father some more, they all heard branches and twigs cracking. Leaves rustling.

The 3 of them turned towards the path. The old fucker grabbed his gun and pointed it at the entrance. Ready to shoot who or whatever was coming through.

The next thing Kelly remembers was racing to the entrance. She doesn't remember how she got there. It felt like she was flying. She didn't remember her feet even touching the ground.

"RONNIE!!!!! OH MY GOD!! RONNIE!!!" All while running.

There he stood. He'd made it to the other side of the path and exactly what he wanted to see he was seeing. His girl, Kelly.

CHAPTER 61

Reunited and It Feels So Good

THEY WERE TOGETHER AND NO ONE was more surprised than Kelly.

"How did you get here? Why did you come? Oh my God, Ronnie, I'm just so happy to see you. You have no idea what I've been through!"

"Hey babe. I flew over. The storm wobbled east and I was able to sneak in. I couldn't stand the thought of you out there in that storm with that asshole Jack."

"He didn't make it, Ronnie. Either did the two boys on the crew. I was all alone out there."

"Jesus, Kelly. I'm so sorry. I should've taken you more seriously. We should've came together. I'm so sorry."

"Oh honey, I'm sorry too. I blew up and made plans I shouldn't have. Captain Jack was my uncle Joe. I found his wallet after he died. He was fathers brother all that time."

"Holy Shit!"

This, of course, would be just one of many stories Kelly would share with Ronnie after the next several hours, but first she felt like she should introduce Selena and her Dad.

"Ronnie this is the nurse that helped get me better after I got beat up."

"Wait a minute ... beat up?? Who beat you up? When?!"

"When I landed here. The cops came and got me and brought me back to the station. They threw me in a cell and later a cop came in and beat the shit out of me. Bad."

"Are you fucking kidding me?!! These asshole cops beat you up? Did they do anything else?!"

The anything else Ronnie spoke of was something else in a very personal nature.

"No. Thank God. But if the chief didn't come in time, he might have."

"The chief helped you?"

"Yes. He brought Selena in to take me to the hospital."

"Who's Selena?

At that Selena stood up and walked over to Ronnie. "I'm Selena. Hello Ronnie. Nice to meet you."

Ronnie was struck by how pretty he thought Selena was. Those eyes of hers were something else. Dark. Deep. He felt like he could see her heart and soul through those eyes.

"Well, hello Miss Selena. Thanks for taking care of my girl."

Kelly had never in all the years she'd been visiting Ronnie heard him call her, publicly, his girl. It thrilled her.

"It was my pleasure. Your "girl" is a wonderful person. We've become quite close."

Ronnie, being the pervert he is, tried picturing that for a second but was shaken out of it by Kelly.

"And this man is my father, Ronnie. Frank Alvarez."

Holy shit, Ronnie thought, he hadn't even noticed him sitting there. He was so damn dirty and disgusting he thought he was part of the camp. Like a tree stump or something.

"Well, Well, Well, if it isn't the asshole Frank Alvarez. Do you have any idea what you've put your daughter through, dickhead?"

"Listen boy, (as Frank reached for his gun) I don't

appreciate being called names. You're standing in my camp. My property. And if you don't change your tone, I'm gonna introduce you to my friend here." Kelly's dad patted the gun.

"Fuck you, old timer! You don't have the balls. Someone who never had the balls to take care of his responsibilities and his family and runs away, couldn't possibly have the balls to do much else. "

"Don't count on that, boy!"

"What, I'm sorry, did you say ROY? Because I don't see any boys standing here!"

Ronnie was now close enough to smell Kelly's dad. And he didn't like the smell. At all. It was something he'd never smelled before.

"Man! Are you one disgusting fucking animal."

Kelly's dad struggled to his feet with one crutch. "Ya know, I don't think I like you."

"I have never liked you, old timer. Now sit the fuck back down before I sit you down for you!"

Ronnie and Kelly's dad were now just a foot away from each other. They just stared at each other. Ronnie was a lot younger than Kelly's dad. And stronger. And faster. He knew this and after a few minutes slowly sat back down, never taking his eyes off Ronnie.

The tension was thick.

"Ronnie, like it or not, this is my dad."

"I don't like it. Not one damn bit."

Kelly had so many questions for her dad. She wanted to know everything. First of all, why did he even get involved with what he got involved with? And then of course why he left. And what has he been doing all these years and most importantly, did he ever think of her.

"But why don't we sit down in this shithole and talk. Kelly I'm guessing you may have some questions for this anim ... I mean man."

Kelly's dad growled at Ronnie.

"I have so many questions I don't know where to start. First of all, why did you get involved with all that illegal stuff?"

Kelly's dad took his eyes off Ronnie and looked at his daughter, "money. That was it, the money was hard to turn away from."

"But you could turn away from your life and family and friends?" A solid question from Kelly.

"I hate you for doing this to me. To us."

Kelly's dad looked at down at the ground. He noticed how dirty he was for the first time. In all these years no one had ever been back here. He never had to worry about how he looked or smelled.

Without lifting his head he said, "I'm so sorry, Kelly."

"I know you can do better than that, Dick head. Apologize to her like you mean it!" said Ronnie.

"I do Fucking mean it! Ok. I'm sorry. I'm sorry we, I mean I fucked up your life, ok?!"

Kelly might have been the only one to catch the "we" in there.

"What do you mean "we"? Do you mean you and Joe"?

"Yea. Me and Joe. That's exactly what I meant."

Kelly wasn't exactly what you'd call "book smart", but she knew people. One good thing she got from her father. She couldn't read a book well, but she could read people. She knew something wasn't right here.

"You and Joe were involved in this, right. Was there someone else?"

"Listen, Kelly, I think there's a lot of explaining to do here."

That was an understatement for sure. Kelly didn't know any of it. At least not the real story.

"Well, I'm listening. I got nowhere else to be."

It took Kelly's dad a long time to look up this time. An uncomfortable amount of time. You could tell he was thinking. Rolling things over in head. Maybe trying to think of the right words. The right way to tell her.

After a way too long pause, Kelly's dad looks up at her, and with tears streaming down his face says, "Honey, my name's not Frank. It's George. Your daddy's big brother."

CHAPTER 62

My Brother's Keeper.

THE THREE PEOPLE THERE AT THIS CAMP in Cuba were all stunned. Their mouths were all hanging open. The disgusting old fucker had just dropped a bombshell.

Kelly was the first to speak.

"My dad didn't have an older brother. He was the oldest."

"No, my dear, I'm the oldest. My parents sent me away a long time before your dad was born. I came back to see him when he was 18. Offered him a job. And he took it. As a matter of fact, he loved it. Loved the money end of it anyway."

"This is crazy bullshit talk! My father never told me about an older brother named George!"

"Of course not, I was doing some bad shit and he got involved. Between the two of us we made a lot of money. I mean, a lot of money. And it was all illegal shit."

"Well if you're my dad's older brother, where is my Dad?"

This was of course an important question. The only question that really mattered. She desperately wanted to know the answer.

She felt so let down now. Here she thought she had found her father and was only talking to an "older brother" she'd met or even heard about. You'd think sometime over the years someone would've known about the older brother George.

Of course, she continued to think, no one knew Captain Jack was her uncle. So, maybe it was possible that no one knew about George.

"Well, where is he? Is he here in Cuba?

Kelly was standing with one hand on her hip and a shitty look in her eye. Ronnie knew that look and the way she was standing. She was between really mad and crying really hard.

"Honey, this is going to be hard to hear. But your Daddy died that day at the courthouse. Full of bullets. In that car."

"NO! That can't be true. Why did Captain, I mean my Uncle Joe, tell me he saw daddy here? Why would he do that?"

"I don't know. I just don't know. I can't answer that."

Ronnie's mouth was still open. He had to consciously close it. He had so many questions himself but figured it best to let Kelly do the talking.

"This doesn't make any sense. You're telling me you're not my dad but another uncle no one has ever heard of and that my other uncle who also had been living a lie tells me my dad is here. Why? Why would any of this be true?"

"Well, I can tell you this, your dad and I made a lot of money. Your uncle too. We squirreled it all away. All of us did. We lived like we're living to just keep adding interest to our accounts. We lived poor. And sacrificed. And because it was all dirty money, the only bank we could keep it at was the one here."

Kelly was shocked to say the least.

"So my father was in that casket?"

"Yea, he was. All those years ago you buried your dad. Your Uncle Joe was always an asshole. Who knows why he lived another life so close to you and kept it from all his life. I suppose part of why he said what he said to you and when he said it, was because he knew he was going to die soon and didn't want you to find out."

"He never told me anything. He was only after he died and I found his license that I figured it out for myself."

"But he got you on the right track. He got you here. To find me."

"Why would I ever want to risk my life to find YOU? I don't even know you. Why would I care?"

"Because I'm the one with all the money, that's why!"

For the second time in the last 20 minutes, everyone visiting the camp had his or her mouths wide open.

"Money. What money? You don't have a dime. Lookit how you're living!"

"Oh there's money alright. And lots of it. I had always hoped that someone would come and find me. Someone who could actually use the money. I could never spend it or enjoy it. I'm a wanted felon. I couldn't go back home. My only hope was that someday someone would come before I die so I could unload it all."

Kelly started to think about all the criminal shit her dad was involved in. Sure there probably was money. Had to be. But she just assumed it was all gone. She lived and grew up pretty poor. If there was so much money, why did dad let everyone suffer?

She asked this question to George.

"We thought it was best that way. Maybe we were wrong, but that's how we did it. We put it all into the bank here and thought by the time someone figured it out there would be millions in there. Of course someone would have to have the key to the box. And there were only 3. One got buried with your Dad, one is at the bottom of the ocean with your Uncle Joe and I have one. The only one left. And now, after all these years, the last one in the family to have enough guts to come looking, would have it.

No one knew how to respond or what to think. Kelly was supposed to believe that this filthy smelly old man had millions in the bank here in Cuba? It didn't seem possible.

She looked over at her newest family member, this man named George. He looked different suddenly. He looked like a man who had finally gotten it all off his chest. Something that he had kept all to himself all these years. A secret. A secret that he told no one.

"So now, I can rest easy. I know now that the family member that's supposed to have the money will now have it. I can die in peace now. It was all worth it to, worth it to see someone like you make this journey as hard as it was for you all worthwhile."

Everyone was looking at George but not really paying attention. Just listening and not really looking.

"I feel so happy. Better than I've felt in 30 years."

George was rubbing his leg. The one he had left. Rubbing and rubbing. He slowly bent over and with the quickest motion imaginable, he grabbed that pistol, put it in his mouth, pointing upwards, and pulled the trigger.

BAM!

"NO!!!!" Yelled by all three of them at the same time. Kelly ran over to him but the sight of him there now bent backwards was too gruesome to look at up close.

"Holy shit! Are you fucking kidding me?" Ronnie was the first one to put a sentence together. "FUCK!" was his also, not really a sentence but appropriate given the circumstances.

Selena who was a devout Christian even chimed in, "Mierda santa!!"

Kelly stood very close to her dead uncle now. It truly was a gruesome sight. His face and the top of his head were just gone. As repulsed as she was, she couldn't stop looking. Her mouth open, hands by her side. Tears running down her cheeks. This was the last man left in her family. Her father, and both uncles, one she didn't even know existed, were all dead. Dead in violent ways.

Her Daddy was killed by assassin bullets, her Uncle Joe was drowned and eaten by a shark and now this one. Uncle George. Uncle Asshole. The one who started all of this had just blown his brains straight out of the top of his head.

"Holy shit!" Ronnie said again.

Ronnie walked over to Uncle Asshole for a closer look. He'd never seen a dead body like this before. Not up close and personal anyway.

He was looking at everything. The whole body. The fatal injury. His old withered body. The spot where his leg used to be. Shit they never found out what happened to his leg! His arms and his wrist especially.

"What is he wearing on his wrist? A bracelet." And a closer look, "A bracelet with a key!"

There was not one thing in this entire camp that had a lock. None of it.

"What the hell do you think that unlocks?" Ronnie asked Kelly.

"I have no idea." Kelly was still shocked from what she saw.

"What if it's a box with money in it? What if it's a box at the bank? Ya think?"

"Yea. Maybe." Kelly had really checked out. She not only had never seen a body up close, she'd never seen one with this kind of injury.

Ronnie started to nose around inside the shelter.

All kinds of worthless shit in here, he thought. But there was one chest. It was beat to hell. Ronnie thought this is it. This is what the key is for. He rushed back out to the old man and without thinking about how gross it was, he pulled the bracelet off the old man and ran back to the chest.

As he got onto all fours, he was quickly discouraged to find there was no working lock on the chest. The key went to something else. Shit, Ronnie thought. "Nothing about this old man is easy is it?"

He opened the chest to find all kinds of books and pads and notebooks and junk that was all decades old. He was just kind of rummaging through it all when he noticed a small book. It was old. He picked it up. It was barely bigger than his own hand. He literally had to dust it off to read what was on the front. After a few seconds of brushing and then rubbing it on his pant leg, he looked at it. He turned it towards what little sunlight was here and opened his mouth wide. Stamped on the front of this little book were the words "BANK OF HAVANA"

"Holy shit!!!" he said once again.

EPILOGUE

IT HAD BEEN QUITE A FEW MONTHS. After the journey to Cuba and back. The discovery of what really happened to her father. Seeing two uncles killed. One by a shark and one by his own hand. It had all been too much to even believe. No one would ever believe this. So Kelly pretty much kept the big stuff to herself. Of course her new husband Ronnie knew.

They had gotten married soon after coming back from Cuba. It took all of that shit they went through to realize they didn't want to be apart ever again. It was a beautiful wedding. As far as they thought anyway. Just the two of them, a minister by the name of Hans and their witness. A witness that witnessed a lot more than them exchanging vows. A witness who seen and helped a lot.

The witness was Selena. She was the only one they could think of. She was family now. They had begged her to move to Key West, but all of her family and her work that she loved were in Cuba.

Hans was a wonderful man and an even better minister. He was a man that had known Kelly's family for a long long time. He even knew Kelly's dad and uncle. Although he never remembered George, he knew the family well enough to be apart of their special day.

Hans was German. Hailing from a small city there called Lahr. He moved to key west 40 years ago. He never looked back or went back. Key west was his home and everyone in town was glad he stuck around.

After visiting the bank of Havana and finding over $25 million US dollars there, they went home in style.

They did everything in style now.

Ronnie was happy with everything. He never thought he would be married, but Kelly was for him. He was also happy that Kelly had all that dough and even more happy that he still had more.

He was busy writing a new book. It was about a family on an island involved in crime and traveling across an ocean to discover long lost treasure.

Sometimes art imitates life.

Sometimes life is a surprise.

And sometimes life sucks

But, more importantly, sometimes life works out exactly as you'd hoped it would.

Thank you for reading.
Please review this book. Reviews help others find
Absolutely Amazing eBooks and inspire us to keep
providing these marvelous tales.

If you would like to be put on our email list to receive
updates on new releases, contests, and promotions,
please go to AbsolutelyAmazingEbooks.com and sign
up.

ABOUT THE AUTHOR

Mark Ryno has been writing radio commercials and checks for over 22 years. He wrote his first book at 12 years old. It was about WWII. His mother didn't like that he used the words hell and damn so much. This is mark's second book, a small novel and he's incredibly proud of it. The most interesting thing about this author is he has written two small novels now, on his iPhone using an App. Born and raised in Upstate New York, Mark has made Key West his home for over 10 years.

ABSOLUTELY AMAZING eBOOKS

AbsolutelyAmazingEbooks.com

or AA-eBooks.com

www.ingramcontent.com/pod-product-compliance
Lightning Source LLC
Chambersburg PA
CBHW061504030726
47503CB00005B/1806